THE STOWAWAYS

Meghan Marentette

With Illustrations by

Dean Griffiths

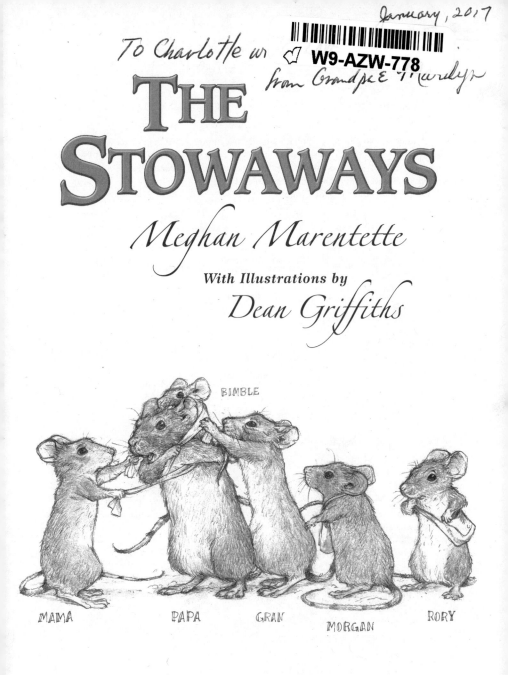

BIMBLE

MAMA   PAPA   GRAN   MORGAN   RORY

pajamapress

Paperback edition first published in Canada and the United States in 2015
First published in the United States in 2014
First Published in Canada in 2013

10 9 8 7 6 5 4 3 2 1

The publisher gratefully acknowledges the support of the Canada Council for the Arts and the Ontario Arts Council for its publishing program. We acknowledge the financial support of the Government of Canada through the Canada Book Fund (CBF) for our publishing activities.

 Canada Council   Conseil des arts
for the Arts   du Canada

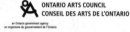 ONTARIO ARTS COUNCIL
CONSEIL DES ARTS DE L'ONTARIO
an Ontario government agency
un organisme du gouvernement de l'Ontario

Canadä

Library and Archives Canada Cataloguing in Publication

Marentette, Meghan, 1974-, author
The stowaways / Meghan Marentette ; illustrations by
Dean Griffiths.

For children ages 8-12.
ISBN 978-1-927485-33-0 (bound) .-978-1-927485-88-0 (pbk.)

I. Griffiths, Dean, 1967-, illustrator II. Title.

PS8626.A7477S76 2013   jC813'.6   C2013-902730-0

Publisher Cataloging-in-Publication Data (U.S.)

Marentette, Meghan, 1974-
The Stowaways / Meghan Marentette.
[240] p. : ill. ; cm.
Summary: Unlike the other Weedle mice, the Stowaways love to go on adventures—even when it means getting close to humans. But when Rory and his Gran plan to rescue Grampa Stowaway, whom everyone else thinks is dead, the adventure becomes dangerous.
ISBN-13: 978-1-927485-33-0
ISBN-13: 978-1-927485-88-0 (pbk.)
1. Mice – Juvenile fiction. 2. Adventure stories. I. Title.
[Fic] dc23   PZ7.M3645St 2013

Cover and interior illustrations–Dean Griffiths
Typesetting and book design–Rebecca Buchanan

Manufactured by Friesens in Altona, Manitoba, Canada in 2015.

Pajama Press Inc.
181 Carlaw Ave. Suite 207 Toronto, ON M4M 2S1
www.pajamapress.ca

Distributed in the United States by Ingram Publisher Services
1 Ingram Blvd. La Vergne, TN 37086, USA

Praise for *The Stowaways*

"In her first novel, Marentette shows promise as a storyteller, creating distinctive characters, building tension, and grounding the fantasy with realistic settings and details. Appearing at intervals throughout the book, Griffiths' lively shaded-pencil drawings capture the personalities of the characters and enhance the charm of the story.... This appealing book will quickly find its audience, fans of mouse adventure tales from George Selden's *The Cricket in Times Square* to Robert C. O'Brien's *Mrs. Frisby and the Rats of NIMH* to Kate DiCamillo's *The Tale of Despereaux*."—**Booklist**

"Themes of courage, family, friendship, and accepting differences permeate the story. Intermittent and well-placed black-and-white illustrations lend a vintage feel to the overall design of the book. A fine debut that deserves a place alongside Cynthia Voigt's *Young Fredle* and Richard Peck's *Secrets at Sea*."—**School Library Journal**

"In the tradition of memorable mouse heroes, the Stowaways deliver page-turning, cliffhanging, heartwarming, first-rate adventure."
—**Kirkus Reviews**

"The clarion call to adventure is irresistible to a certain kind of mouse. Not since Stuart Little has the heart of a valiant mouse beat quite so fiercely as that of Rory Stowaway in Meghan Marentette's first novel, *The Stowaways*. It meets and exceeds all the expectations of a good mouse story, with a well-constructed and self-sufficient mouse world, a teeny-tiny hero set against impossible odds, and an adventure brimming with mystery that scampers from chapter to chapter."—**The National Reading Campaign**

"...this book is charming, exciting, interesting, and really good fun. I hesitate to compare it to *The Wind in the Willows*, but it is in the same league; so read and enjoy. I especially recommend it as a read-aloud for those younger ones who would hesitate to tackle a 200-pager on their own, but will love hearing the story. Highly Recommended."—**CM Magazine**

For my parents
—M.M.

For George
—D.G.

✤ONE✤

A LEGEND TO UPHOLD

Through the relentless rain and fog of that dreary, cold spring, Rory was completely miserable. He couldn't find anything fun to do. His brother Morgan, his older twin by one and a half *long* minutes, was much better at occupying himself—he could make all kinds of toys and useful things out of scraps of wood and plastic. But Rory wasn't good with his paws, and Morgan knew it. Between his confident smirks, he loved to remind Rory of his lesser age, wisdom, and skill.

Normally, Rory didn't mind. He knew his own life was meant for adventure, and that's where his thoughts always roamed. After all, the Stowaways had always been known as great explorers and he was sure that one day *he* would become a brave adventurer like his ancestors. Only one thing stood in his way—their father.

Papa refused to take his sons exploring, no matter how much they asked. Morgan simply accepted the denials but Rory could never let it go. He would argue that Gran and Grampa used to take *Papa* on adventures when *he* was young. And when that didn't work, he'd say that pretty soon the Stowaways' fame would be forgotten if they didn't keep exploring. But that argument in particular only made matters worse. Papa wouldn't budge.

So Rory tried to persuade Gran, instead. She always had a mischievous twinkle in her eye when she talked of her old adventures—maybe *she* would take them somewhere. But Rory couldn't convince Gran either, since Grampa had gone missing on a journey, long ago. She told Rory firmly that her traveling days were over.

So Rory was stuck in the fog with a know-it-all brother and a strict father who insisted they go no farther than the path between their house and school. And for a mouse with itchy feet, this was wholly discouraging.

But today felt different to Rory. He woke with a strange, fluttery hope in his chest—like a little hand of excited fingers was about to pluck him out of the gloom. Maybe the sun would tear through the fog, their teacher would finally close school for the summer, and Papa would take them somewhere new!

His belly twisted anxiously at breakfast. He ate only one paw-ful of porridge and even sacrificed his mother's special Juneberry paste, just to get outside faster.

But when Rory opened the door, hope faded quickly.

Blue jays squawked and swished in the reeds nearby and Weedle River gurgled noisily behind him, but Rory couldn't see much at all beyond his whiskers. Thick fog crept up the hill and over the puddles to his soggy, cold paws. He tied his scarf around his neck and sighed. When would summer ever come?

"What time is it?" Morgan was already outside, propping up their little sister's play-tent in order to repair a hole in the sagging roof. He held a thin reed between his teeth.

Rory sloshed over to the sundial in the middle of their yard. With his claws, he scraped the mushy pollen out of the hour-line grooves, then carefully wiped a drop of rain off the tip of the gnomon, the upright part that cast a shadow over the hour lines to show the time. He liked to keep the sundial clean for Gran—she had carved it herself out of soapstone and made the gnomon from a falcon's talon his grandfather had broken off during a daring escape. Rory wished Grampa was still around—*he* would take them on adventures.

"Well? Is it time to go, or what?" said Morgan.

The shadow of the talon was faint and hard to read, but Rory thought it might be somewhere near nine o'clock. "Hard to say," he said with a deep sigh. "It's never sunny enough to tell."

Morgan turned an ear toward the sky as he used the reed to sew up the hole in the tent. "You're such a downer, Ror. Look at that bright patch up there—I bet you Miss Creemore ends school today and Papa takes us on an adventure tomorrow!"

Rory twitched his ears angrily. "You think you know everything! Papa won't even let us help scavenge at Biggle's farm. What makes you think he'll suddenly take us somewhere?"

"Gran will make him."

"But she won't even go herself! How can you say that?"

"I heard her talking secretly to Mama last night about going to the World Beyond."

"No way—that's where Papa says Terrible Things happen. He'd never let any of us go there!" But Rory's hope was already swelling again. "What else did she say?"

"I don't know—some mouse came back from there recently, or something. And now Gran really wants to go."

"You're lying!" Rory couldn't believe it. No Weedle Mouse outside their family had ever gone beyond Biggle's farm, and only Grampa had gone past the towns of Eekum and Seekum. And besides, Gran insisted she would never go on an adventure again without Grampa. If only he would come home, then everyone could go exploring again. "Do you think Grampa will ever come back?"

"*No*, Rory. How many times do I have to tell you? Papa said Grampa was caught in a trap and is never coming back."

"It still seems kind of strange that he'd be trapped so easily. He escaped a falcon once, after all. Gran said—"

"Gran spins a lot of tales, Rory. Grampa is dead and gone. Grow up."

"You're mean!"

"Well at least I'm not *bor*ing like you. Believe what you want, but I know we're going on an adventure this summer. We are the *Stowaways*." Morgan tied a knot in the reed and chewed off the end.

"I hope you're right." Rory gave up the argument and leaned on the sundial with his elbows, his cheeks in his paws.

If there was one thing that united the brothers, it was pride in their ancestry. Gran always said their family came from a long line of bold explorers, and the twins were glad they had inherited the desire to travel. But many seasons had passed without a journey, now. Rory thought he could remember going somewhere once… but since his parents never talked of old adventures anymore, all he was left with was a yearning to go back, wherever it was.

Morgan came up behind him. "Why didn't you say it was almost nine? We're going to be late!" He smacked Rory's ear and began to run.

"Ow!" Rory lunged sideways and grabbed Morgan's tail, but his paw slipped off his brother's wet fur and he lost his balance, falling flat on his face. Mud oozed between his clenched teeth. He was furious.

Morgan laughed as he ran down the hill. "Last one to the bottom's a dirty rat!"

Rory shook the mud off his whiskers and scrambled to his feet to race after Morgan. But before he could find his balance, he fell straight back down again—only this time he fell onto a lucky piece of cellophane his parents had scavenged the day before. It made a perfect sled.

"Hey, slowpoke! Think you're so fast now?" Rory slid rapidly over the wet grass, passing Morgan halfway down the hill.

Morgan watched in disbelief as his brother zoomed by.

"Hey! Wait for me!" he yelled.

But Rory couldn't stop. The sled carried him faster and faster down the hill until he finally came to a bumpy halt, where the grass disappeared into the rocks of an old, dry streambed.

Long ago, the streambed had flowed with runoff water from the pond at Biggle's farm, down the bank toward Weedle River. But the farm added always-thirsty goats to the pasture, and the pond was never full anymore. Now the old streambed made a clear path through a cranberry bog and up the bank toward school.

Rory wished he could go off the path and explore the bog. He picked up a pebble and threw it into the reeds, listening to the *ploop* as it fell into a puddle.

"*Squawk!*" A blue jay suddenly flew up and away. Rory jolted in surprise and dived behind a rock. He'd never been so close to a bird before. Papa told them birds ate mice and they were forbidden to go near them. But did *every* size of bird eat mice? He wondered.

Morgan finally caught up, breathing heavily.

"Took you long enough," said Rory, teasing.

Morgan bent over, pretending to be exhausted. "What are you sitting there for, lazy bones?" He suddenly raced off again.

"Hey!" cried Rory, running after him.

The brothers chased each other along the streambed, balancing and scrabbling over the pebbles. Rory was about to pull ahead of Morgan when he stepped on the end of his own scarf, yanking it tight around his neck. He stopped on his haunches to adjust it.

"Watch out!" cried Morgan. A blue jay dived across the path, nicking Rory's ear with its wing.

"Whoa!" said Rory, ducking.

The bird landed in the path ahead and screeched fiercely.

"Hide!" Morgan pulled Rory behind a rock with him. Another jay landed, squawking wildly at the other one. "We'd better stay out of sight. They look angry."

"Shh! Listen." Rory's ears rose like two furry moons over the rock.

"They stashed a pile of seeds on a raft and tied it to a reed in a bog pool.... Last night the wind bent the reed over, the tie slipped off, and the raft floated away."

"So? What do I care?" said Morgan, pulling Rory down again. "Papa said we're not allowed to talk to birds."

"We don't have to talk to them," said Rory. "If we find their stash first, we can take some home to Gran. She'll be proud!"

Morgan paused for a second, considering his brother's scheme.

"We're late enough for school as it is," he said finally.

"Look, there they go! C'mon!" Rory leapt over the rock and ran past Morgan, ignoring the puddles and drenching himself.

"Wait!" Morgan ran after him, his voice wobbling as he bounced over the rough ground and off the path, into the bog. "You're going to get us lost!"

Rory rolled nose over hind feet as he tore after the birds, listening for the *swish*, *swish* of their wings through the reeds before dashing off again.

"We're not supposed to be in here! You'll get us in trouble."

"Who's *bor*ing now?" Rory yelled back at his brother.

Morgan stopped, annoyed. "I hope those birds *eat* you before you get their seeds!"

He began to run after Rory again, but it was too late. The fog had swallowed Rory up, and he was gone.

"You're going to get us lost!"

TWO

FORBIDDEN FRIENDS

Rory raced after the jays. He bounded between tufts of grass and patchy gravel in the dank mud of the bog. Finally the birds landed, chirping excitedly—they had spotted their raft. Rory stopped and waited for Morgan, but minutes passed and his brother still didn't appear. He climbed up a tall rock to see better, but at the top he soon realized that not only had he lost Morgan, he'd lost the path too.

The dull tinkle of metal chimes sounded in the distance. Rory's ears perked up. The school bell! He turned around and around, desperate to figure out which direction the sound was coming from, but it ended before he could tell. He was lost.

Rory sighed in defeat and slid back down the rock, where he sat slumped at its base and watched the jays from a safe distance.

They were arguing over their raft—a piece of driftwood, piled high with thistle seeds. It had floated into the middle of a deep rain pool and jammed itself between two steep rocks that jutted out of the water. One bird was precariously perched on the rock slope, trying to poke the raft free with its wing, but its feathers kept brushing over the seed pile and knocking the precious food into the water.

"You'll never get it that way!" cried the second bird from shore. "Fly at the raft and try to push it through!"

"No, it'll flip over and sink all the seeds!"

"Well *you* think of something, then!"

"I'm trying, but I can't think while you're screeching at me!"

The jays squawked rowdily until one flew away in a rage and all became quiet.

Rory picked up a twig in his paw and began to draw a map in the sandy gravel at his feet as he tried to retrace his steps. But it was hopeless—his mind wandered and his map became a mess of aimless circles. What would Papa say when he found out he went off the path? What if he was lost forever? He would miss home so much—Morgan and his little sister Bimble playing by the fire, Mama making a fresh batch of Juneberry juice, Papa and Gran sitting nearby, laughing about past adventures, just like old times....

"Drawing a pretty picture, are we?"

Rory jumped to his feet. The remaining blue jay was standing over him.

"Stay back!" cried Rory. He held up the twig and pointed it at the bird.

The jay drew himself up, puffed out his feathers, and aimed his sharp beak down at Rory, like a sword. Rory tried to fluff out his fur, but he was still wet from the puddles. He looked more pathetic than scary.

The jay bent down with his head cocked to one side, his beady black eye nearly touching Rory's nose. "What are you doing here? Speak up!"

Sweat began to creep through Rory's fur. He'd never been face-to-face with a bird before and had certainly never talked to one—that was *strictly* forbidden. He suddenly wondered if he was about to experience one of the Terrible Things that Papa said would happen in the World Beyond. His whiskers began to quiver and his knees began to knock until his whole body shook, even the twig in his paw.

"My g-grandfather once escaped a falcon a thousand times your size!" he finally spluttered.

"*Ooh*," said the jay, mocking him. "A bird a thousand times my size could hardly fly, but nice try." The jay stood tall again and squinted down at Rory. "I won't eat you if you make me a deal."

Rory didn't like the sound of that. Every time Morgan made "a deal" with him, he always ended up losing out.

"There's n-nothing you can d-do for me," said Rory.

"Hmmm." The jay relaxed his feathers into place and smoothed out his chest with a wing. "You do look a little lost, but I guess *I* can't help you with that." He turned to fly away.

"Er...well, I am late for school, but I'm not—no, definitely not really *lost*. I was just trying to—"

The jay swung back around and spread out his wings. "Steal my seeds!" he bellowed. "I saw you follow me!"

Rory was so startled that he dropped the twig. "I just wanted to b-bring some home for my family!"

The jay took a deep breath and puffed up his chest. "So you thought rather than find your own seeds, you'd take mine and save yourself the trouble?"

Rory stared at his feet.

"Well, it looks like you're in *trouble* now!"

Rory wondered how Grampa could possibly have escaped a falcon when even a blue jay could be this frightening.

"Shall we entertain my deal then?" continued the jay.

"O-okay."

"What's your name?"

"Rory Stowaway, sir."

"Aren't you going to ask mine?"

Rory looked up. The jay's eyes sparkled as he made a low, graceful bow.

"My name is Glee. Don't you know jays dislike the taste of mice?"

"No, sir."

"Well, it's true. Your ears are far too tough, and all that fur gets caught in the throat."

Rory gulped.

"I'm just kidding—I've never tasted mouse. I prefer the soft squish of slugs!" Glee laughed heartily.

Relieved, Rory smiled. He wasn't going to be eaten after all.

"I'm sorry I went after your seeds, Mr. Glee. If you show me where the path is, I'll help you however I can."

His good manners appeared to impress the bird. "I need to set my raft free," Glee said, pointing to the rocks. "Your deft little paws may be just what I need."

Rory couldn't help thinking that Gran would approve of this adventure, no matter what Papa said. He picked up his twig again and tapped it on the ground as he thought of a plan.

"Can you lift me?" he asked Glee.

"Well, I suppose I could, by that scarf around your neck. But I don't want to hurt you."

"We'll practice over dry ground first," said Rory, gaining confidence. He gnawed at the twig until it was flat at one end and round at the other, like a paddle. With a mouthful of pulp, he mumbled excitedly, "I'll stay down on all fours, and you fly over me."

"Okay…but I don't see how we'll get the raft free." Glee flew up overhead.

Rory clutched the twig in his mouth and waited, nervous but determined. If Grampa could survive the claws of a bird, so could he.

Glee swooped down and grabbed Rory's scarf in his claws. As he flew up again, the scarf grew tighter around Rory's neck and he swung back and forth like a pendulum in the air.

"Stop! Stop!" choked Rory.

Glee stopped flapping and slowly lowered Rory to the ground. Rory loosened his scarf quickly and gasped for air.

"Er…I guess that didn't work," said Glee. The yarn was still caught in his claws. He held up his feet one at a time while Rory untangled the yarn.

"You've got to be able to pick me up firmly, so I don't swing." Rory took in a few long breaths, thinking harder. "If I take off my scarf, you could pick me up by the scruff of my neck, as if…as if you were a—"

"Falcon?" said Glee, shuffling his feet nervously.

Rory swallowed. "Yeah. But fly me over to the raft and drop me onto it. Don't eat me." He tried to smile.

"No more dry runs?"

"If all goes well, this *will* be a dry run—that pool looks really deep." Rory took off his scarf, relieved to rid himself of the damp mass of wool. A warm breeze swept through his matted neck fur. He was going to make Gran proud.

Glee flew up into position again. Rory clenched the twig in his mouth and listened for the sound of the bird's wings flapping and swooping down hard. As the sound grew stronger in his ears— *whooh, whooh, whooh*—he had to fight his instinct to run away.

Glee was nearly at the ground when he lifted his head, reached out with his claws, and clutched Rory's neck. He flapped his wings to balance himself and then headed straight for the raft, flying low over the pool.

Rory's hind feet trailed in the water, leaving a rippled wake behind them. He was trying not to think about drowning, when the raft was suddenly beneath him.

"Now! Drop me now!" Glee released his claws and Rory fell hard on the front edge of the raft, which rocked violently under his weight. Seeds went flying over his head and into the water.

"Phew!" said Rory, flicking a seed off his head. He looked up to find Glee, but the sun glared in his eyes. The sun was breaking through the fog at last! He *knew* something great would happen today. He crawled around the pile of seeds to the back of the raft, where it was stuck between the rocks.

Glee landed on a rock above and called down to him through cupped wings. "How are you going to free it?"

Rory didn't answer. He nudged the rock on his left with the twig and the raft pushed forward slightly. Then he switched to the right side and nudged the other rock. The raft moved forward a little more. With two more pushes and one giant shove, the raft finally lurched forward. Rory paddled furiously with the flat end of the twig, switching from left to right with each stroke, straining to see where he was going over the pile of seeds. Before long the raft came to a halt in the mud, and he scampered off to shore.

"Hooray!" cried Glee, landing beside Rory. "You did it!"

Rory's heart thumped with excitement. Victory! He lay down

to rest, closing his eyes in the warm sun. But as he calmed down, the feeling he had forgotten something took over and he began to panic. He leapt to his feet.

"Morgan!"

"If that's who I saw you with earlier," said Glee soberly, "he left when you went off the path."

Rory was relieved that his brother wasn't lost, too, but felt hurt at being abandoned. Morgan never wanted to do anything unless it was his own idea.

"I'll show you out now," said Glee, patting Rory's back with his wing.

Rory followed the jay, who hopped from reed to reed, waiting for him to catch up. Soon the path appeared and they stopped to say goodbye.

"Thank you, Mr. Glee."

"It's you who should be thanked."

Rory watched Glee's white-tipped wings flap away in the sun. He couldn't wait to tell Gran about his new friend. But first he would have to get through the school day. He scurried up the hill to the grove of trees outside the fence that surrounded Biggle's farm. At the base of an old oak tree, he took a deep breath before entering a tall, dark hollow.

✖ THREE ✖

DETENTION

The Weedle Mice School was hidden in the base of an ancient oak tree, near the fence that surrounded Biggle's goat pasture. The entrance to the hollow was shaped like a witch's hat—tall and triangular, with a heavy goat-hair curtain draped across it, to keep out the chill and snow.

Inside, wooden pillars lined the room to support a low ceiling of crisscrossed branches. Acorn lanterns hung from the branches over each of thirty desks, which Miss Creemore had made out of flat wooden spoons from the ice-cream stand at Biggle's petting zoo. Behind her desk, a flat piece of slate leaned against the wall, which she wrote on with a shard of chalk and wiped off with the fur of her elbow.

This morning's lesson was multiplication. Miss Creemore stood on her hind legs behind her desk, as she always did to emphasize her authority, and presented a walnut shell full of thistle seeds. As she called out math questions, she threw seeds to the mice who answered correctly. It was everyone's favorite game, but Morgan wasn't participating.

He slumped down on his little log bench and glared at the door-way. He was *glad* he'd left Rory behind when he ran off the trail. When Miss Creemore had asked where his brother was, Morgan wished he had just told her the truth and let Rory suffer the conse-quences. Where *was* he, anyway?

Just then, Rory poked his head around the edge of the curtain. He looked wet and his scarf was missing. He crept into the room as quietly as he could, unseen by Miss Creemore as the math game had reached a roaring level of excitement. Almost all the students were up off their benches, reaching for flying seeds. Rory took his place at the desk beside Morgan.

"Where *were* you?" whispered Morgan angrily.

"I was talking to that bird," Rory said quietly.

"What? We're not supposed to talk to birds!"

"*Shh!*" Rory lowered his voice. "I had to—I was lost and I needed his help."

"Papa will be angry," said Morgan, trying not to sound envious.

"Don't tell him. Please?"

"Fine," pouted Morgan. "But I've already covered for you once today."

"Thanks. But no thanks for leaving me!" Rory whispered back so fiercely that Wally, who sat on his other side, took notice.

"Miss Creemore!" said Wally. "Rory's here and he's talking to Morgan during class *again*." The mouse looked over at Rory and stuck out his tongue.

Miss Creemore stopped the lesson abruptly and raised her paw. Everyone sat down. "Thank you for the information, Wally. Why don't you put your tongue back in your head and save us the view of it? *That*'s better, thank you." She turned to Rory. "I thought you were ill. You do look a bit sweaty. Are you sure you should be here?"

Rory's ears turned a darker shade of pink as all eyes turned on him. "I—um, well, I felt better so I thought I should come," he said. "Did you know the sun is out?" he added, hoping to change the subject.

Everyone turned toward the door and then back to Miss Creemore, eagerly awaiting her response.

"That can wait," she said sternly. "Why are you wet?"

"It's a long story."

"I see. Then you will stay after school and refill the lanterns while you tell me all about it."

"Yes, Miss Creemore," mumbled Rory.

Morgan smiled at his brother tauntingly. Refilling the lanterns was the worst chore. Rory would have to melt a candle stub into a bucket with a lit match, climb up on each desk, pour the hot wax into the lantern, and then hold the wick straight as the wax cooled—all while balancing on his hind legs—thirty separate times.

But Rory was thankful he wouldn't have to explain what had happened in the bog in front of the whole class. The Stowaways were already ridiculed for being "different" from other Weedle Mice and he knew such a story would only make it worse. He'd never heard of a mouse talking to a bird before and he didn't want to find out whether he would be admired or mocked.

Miss Creemore continued the math lesson and the students jumped up off their benches again, yelling out numbers and catching seeds. Wally kicked Rory's bench and it rolled back, forcing Rory to grab the edge of his desk to keep his balance.

"What were you doing out there, weirdo? Drowning in a raindrop?"

Rory's ears burned but he kept quiet.

Morgan leaned behind his brother's back and scoffed at Wally. "Only you would do something as stupid as that. I saw you last week in obstacle class—you couldn't even jump over a four-inch puddle!"

"Yeah? Well at least I don't smell of garbage!" said Wally.

"Better than living in an empty hole like you!"

"At least we're not trying to be townies like your stinkin' family."

"How would you know? You've never been to town before—you wouldn't know a townie if one hit you!"

"You're gonna hit me?" said Wally, misunderstanding. He leaned closer to Morgan, so the two were nose to nose behind Rory's back. Rory rolled closer to his desk, away from their hot breath.

"I wouldn't waste my energy," said Morgan. He sat upright again and began to pick imaginary dirt out of his claws, quite unaffected.

Rory looked anxiously at Morgan. His brother had a talent for disturbing the peace, taking every chance he could to brag about their family's explorations and the things they made out of materials the Humans threw away. Rory avoided other Weedle Mice—many of them were rough, rustic creatures who sneered at the Stowaways' curiosity and invention.

Wally looked furious as he appeared to slowly digest Morgan's insult. Finally he spat out, "Why don't you meet me outside after school—then we'll figure out who's better!"

"It would take forever for you to figure something out," Morgan replied, pretending to look bored.

"Stop encouraging him, Morgan!" whispered Rory. "Papa will have your head if something happens—and then we'll never get to go on an adventure!"

Wally overheard. "What do you snobs do on your little adventures, anyway?"

"Nothing a brute like you would understand," said Morgan.

Wally rose up off his bench, incensed.

"Wally!" cried Miss Creemore. The class was suddenly silent as they fell back on their benches.

"Wally, what is two multiplied by three?" Miss Creemore waited but he didn't reply. "I *asked* you a question," she insisted.

Wally sighed loudly and finally spoke. "I don't know, Miss. But I do know there are two Stowaways in this room who are going to regret it when they meet my big brother Dill and my friends Mack and Jack after school."

Rory flinched. Mack and Jack were older orphan brothers who

never went to school. He heard they lived in the bog somewhere on a human toy boat, but he'd never seen them, and he didn't want to meet them now.

"Aha!" said Miss Creemore. "So there will be three groups of two brothers meeting after school. And how many mice is that?"

Wally furrowed his brow. "Six?"

"Precisely!" said Miss Creemore. "Three groups of two—or two multiplied by three—is six. Thank you for illustrating this to the class." She threw Wally a seed, which bounced off his head and landed at his feet. "And since you are so obliging, you'll stay after school to sweep the floor." She glared at him until he sat down.

Morgan smiled triumphantly while Rory slouched down and sank his face into his paws. Now Wally would be in detention with him. *Thanks a lot*, he mouthed at Morgan.

The other students broke out in whispers, betting on who would win a fight between Wally and Rory. Rory began to feel nauseated.

Miss Creemore banged a gavel on the desk and silence resumed.

"Well! Rory's news that the sun has appeared is welcome indeed. So, I'm letting you out early today. And…" She paused, smiling widely as the students fidgeted. "This will be the last day of school. Summer season has begun!" Squeals broke out across the room and everyone leapt up and cheered. Miss Creemore laughed as she moved toward the door. "I look forward to seeing you all in the fall. Class dismissed!" She pulled aside the curtain and the sun shone brilliantly through the hollow.

Everyone jumped on their desks, blew out their lanterns, and scurried toward the door, where they arranged themselves in a line. Miss Creemore shook the paw of each mouse and remarked on his or her good behavior and efforts that year. The students thanked her politely but impatiently, longing to get outside in the sun.

When it was Morgan's turn to say goodbye, Miss Creemore held onto his paw a little longer. "You're a smart young whip, but don't be too sure you will always avoid trouble. And remember, an arrogant mouse is a lonely one." Morgan grunted in alleged agreement. "Say hello to your mother for me and tell her your sister may start school this fall. I can see she is just as clever as you are, so it's time we began training her to use those smarts *wisely*."

Morgan scampered off with a smile on his face. Having Bimble at school would be terrifically entertaining!

Rory watched his brother go in dismay. He could feel Wally's eyes burn into the back of his head.

When the last student was gone, Miss Creemore marched back to her desk. "Well then, Wally, there's the broom." She pointed to an altered toothbrush leaning against the wall, then handed Rory a walnut shell bucket with a wire handle and directed him toward a pile of candle stubs. "Get melting."

She cleared her desk of seeds and began to write student progress reports with a fat pencil stub. As she finished each one, she filed them into matchbox drawers under her desk. She did not look up.

Rory lit a match and began to melt the candle stubs, letting the wax drip into the bucket. Wally grabbed the broom. As he passed by Rory, he poked him hard in the ribs with the handle. Rory fumbled and nearly splashed wax on himself, but he continued to ignore Wally, hoping he would just sweep quickly and leave.

When Rory was finished melting the wax, he climbed onto a desk to fill the first lantern. Wally half-heartedly swept some seeds into a pile nearby.

"Don't fall, pack rat!" Wally sneered and bumped his broom forcefully against the desk leg. The desk wobbled as Rory tried to keep his balance. Miss Creemore cleared her throat warningly but stayed focused on her work.

Wally lowered his voice to a sharp whisper. "Did Biggle's cat get your tongue? Can't say anything, loser?"

Rory flared his nostrils. He could feel his temper begin to rise as he looked down at Wally.

"Your brother can't help you now!" Wally jabbed the broom at Rory's legs. Rory pulled his foot back, just dodging the attack. Wax spilled out of his bucket and splashed on his bare paw. With a quick grimace and a jolt of rage, he poured the rest of the wax directly on Wally's head.

"*Ye*-ouch!" squealed Wally. "You dirty, rotten rat!" He was about to swipe at Rory again but was suddenly unable to move— Miss Creemore had crossed the room quietly and now stood on

Wally's tail. He immediately dropped the broom.

"Rory Stowaway, come down here at once."

Rory's heart thumped. Miss Creemore was angry. He scrambled off the desk and stood before her, looking nervously at her twitching tail. It was extraordinarily long, with many dark stripes.

She extended a claw as she pointed at a bench. "Sit. Down. Now. Both of you." Rory and Wally obeyed. "I am extremely disappointed," she continued. "What do you two have to say for yourselves?"

Neither mouse replied.

"All right, then. Rory—you've managed to give Wally a fine wax hat. Go get the knife and cut it out of his fur." Rory and Wally both stood up, shocked.

"You really want me to cut his fur?" said Rory.

"That's right. Go get the knife from the bottom drawer of my desk." Rory fetched the old, rusty razor blade and returned to Wally, who sat down slowly on the bench. With her tail, Miss Creemore flicked a thread spool out from the wall, and it landed at Rory's feet. "Stand on that."

Rory climbed on the spool and positioned the blade over Wally's head. Trying desperately to keep his paws steady, he slowly cut out the messy glops of fused wax and fur and dropped them to the floor. Wally sat perfectly still, his eyes crossed as he looked up nervously. Miss Creemore stood silently over them. When Rory was finished, she held out her paw and he gave her the blade. Wally patted the bald spots on his head in disbelief.

"Now finish your chores. *Peacefully.*"

Rory and Wally scurried back to bucket and broom, staying well away from each other. Wally finished first. Miss Creemore inspected his work, shook his paw firmly, and told him he would do better to spend his energy learning than bullying. He lumbered out the door, still groping at his head.

Rory was slow to finish, as he had to re-melt the wax. He finally climbed down from the last desk and approached Miss Creemore.

"Sorry I was late today. I got lost in the bog…on an adventure." He couldn't help feeling a little proud of himself.

Rory climbed on the spool and positioned the blade over Wally's head.

Miss Creemore put down her pencil.

"You're much like your grandfather, aren't you?"

"I am?" Rory smiled, glad of the comparison.

"He was itchier to explore than your father ever was. Like you." She smiled as she scratched her cheek with her claw. "When we were young, he used to go off on daring adventures with his sister Hazel, your great-aunt—" Miss Creemore broke off and stood up abruptly, as if she suddenly remembered something important. "You'll say hello to your grandmother for me, won't you?"

"You were going to say something!"

"Yes, er…say hello to your parents too. And, here—take this for them." She pushed a bucket of seeds in his paw.

"Do *you* know what happened to Grampa?" Rory persisted as he followed her to the doorway. "Is he in the World Beyond? Will he ever come back? Gran says she knows he will."

"If only she would come around…," she whispered. Before Rory could ask another question, she pushed him outside. "Now run off home. Keep your temper in check and your brother close. You'll need each other one day."

As Rory left, he saw Wally and his brother Dill waiting by the fence. Rory sped toward the old streambed and ran as fast as he could, though rather clumsily with the bucket of seeds in one paw. He expected them to chase him, but Wally only laughed.

"I'll get you back, rat. Don't you worry!"

FOUR

RELEASE

When Rory reached the top of their hill, he found Morgan dancing with Bimble around the sundial. The afternoon sun gleamed through her large pink ears, which flapped like flags around her face.

"I go schoo-ool!" she sang over and over.

Rory smiled, glad to be home.

Gran was sunbathing on the lounge chair Morgan had made out of twigs. The fur on her belly glowed white in the sun, and her long tail coiled like a snake in her lap. Rory thought she looked worried; her whiskers were twitchy and more crooked than usual. He put the bucket of seeds down beside her.

"Here's the tardy one," said Gran, passing him a Juneberry. "Bimble and I picked these this morning. Did you know she could already climb? Her crib won't hold her in now!" Though she looked proudly at Bimble, Rory noticed she could barely form a smile. Something wasn't right.

Rory put the berry in his mouth and made a sour face.

"Gran!" he said, spitting it out. "They aren't ripe yet!"

"All the better to grow fur on your feet."

Morgan ran over to Rory's bucket of seeds and took one. "Are these the seeds you took from that bird?" He gobbled it down.

"You did *what*?" Gran sat up.

"Morgan, you said you wouldn't tell!"

"No, I said I wouldn't tell *Papa*."

"And you'd better not," said Gran, glaring at Morgan.

"Anyway, you're not supposed to talk to birds," scolded Morgan.

"You *talked* to it?" Gran's face lit up.

Rory nodded, wishing he could have told her first.

"Birds will kill you," said Morgan.

"Not this one. He was kind of funny, actually," said Rory.

Gran stroked her chin. "Interesting..."

"Boddle!" yelled Bimble as she buried a piece of broken glass in the flowerbed. Morgan laughed and ran over to explain that glass doesn't grow into bottles. He showed her how to plant a thistle seed instead.

Gran lowered her voice. "Be careful, Rory. You know the story of your grandfather and the falcon." She poked his belly. "Not all birds are kind." She lay back again and smiled. "If only Grampa knew what you did!"

Rory puffed out the fur on his chest. Gran was impressed.

Mama and Papa appeared in the yard with their daily haul from Biggle's farm, where they spent every morning, rifling through the waste bins. They always brought home a surprising pile of food and treasures: old bread, mouldy cheese ("Extra protein", Gran would say), broken tiles, toothbrushes, paper clips, pencil stubs, crumpled foil, and scraps of yarn, newspaper, cardboard, and tattered cloth—anything and everything. Even their wheelbarrow was made from human cast-offs—half an old cough-drop tin fixed to a button wheel.

"Beautiful day," said Papa, wiping his brow. He looked greasy with sweat.

"Hmpf," said Gran, looking away.

So Gran is mad at Papa, thought Rory. *Well, that isn't entirely unusual.*

"You boys are home early," said Mama.

"Miss Creemore called summer break today!" Morgan and Bimble ran over to the wheelbarrow. "What'd you get?"

"A new porridge pot," said Mama. She pulled out a thimble.

"Where did you find that?" said Morgan.

Mama giggled and looked sideways at Papa. "It fell off the windowsill at Biggle's farmhouse…and landed on Papa's head. It stuck over his cheeks—I had to grease him with some old butter wrap to get it off!"

Papa wiped his face again as everyone laughed. "Shall we go in for dinner?" he said, trying to hide his smile. As he went inside the house, Gran immediately followed.

Morgan and Bimble stayed outside to play while Rory helped Mama organize their haul. They stored the bulk of it in the cellar outside (a cave dug under the house) and took the food and thimble inside.

The Stowaways' home was two equal-sized rooms joined by a wide archway. In the living room, the family could sit by the fire or sleep in their beds, which were placed in each corner. In the kitchen, a simple counter and cupboards lined one wall, and in the far corner, a pantry room extended out from the house. Directly opposite the fireplace in the living room sat the cooking hearth in the kitchen, with the dining table nearby.

Mama hung the thimble with the other pots and pans on a wire garland over the hearth and carried the food to the pantry.

"So you didn't think about what I said last night, then?" Gran stood over Papa as he washed his face in the sink. Nobody noticed Rory, who sat quietly at the table.

"Mother, that's enough—they're too young! And what about Bimble? We can't carry her everywhere."

"Your father used to strap you on his back when you were her age. Or don't you remember?"

"Are we going somewhere?" Rory could hardly hear himself over the excited thumping in his chest. No one else seemed to hear him either.

Mama brought the last of the winter walnuts to the table. "Oh, come on. We can at least go to Eekum." She patted her husband's cheek.

"I'll think about it," said Papa.

"Don't think too long," said Gran. "We don't have much time."

"What you want to do is too dangerous!"

"Well, I can always go alone," Gran said testily.

Papa pushed the window open over the sink. "Morgan!" he called. "Bring Bimble in. It's time to eat."

Gran frowned at her son. "You always change the subject, don't you?" She sat down next to Rory, who looked at her curiously.

What was that all about? he thought.

Morgan ran in with Bimble on his back. He deposited her next to Gran and sat across from Rory.

Rory spoke up again, louder this time. "Are we going somewhere?"

"Not if your father can help it," said Gran.

Morgan's ears perked up. "You're taking us on an adventure?"

"When you grow into those ears a little more, maybe," said Papa, sitting down. "Now pass me that paper."

Rory slid a newspaper cutting across the table as he studied Papa's ears. Young and old Weedle Mice had the same sized ears. As they matured, their ears appeared smaller, since adult heads were so much bigger in comparison. Rory wondered when his ears would look small enough for him to be allowed on an adventure.

"My ears are smaller than *yours*," said Morgan, teasing Rory. Rory shrugged. Morgan's thicker body did make his ears look smaller, but Rory was just glad they weren't identical twins. He had a slight build with gray fur like Mama and Bimble. Morgan was more like Papa and Gran—sturdy and brown.

"How long was Grampa's tail?" asked Rory, ignoring Morgan. It was a question he'd asked many times, but he liked to hear Gran talk about the rarity of their breed. He often checked his tail fur, looking for a new stripe that would appear with every growth spurt and then darken with age. Gran claimed the stripes grew in with every stage of wisdom—and that's why her tail was so long.

"Well," said Gran. "Your grandfather's tail is *so* long that he can carry a whole croissant, coiled up in his tail, all the way back from Eekum!"

"You mean he *used to* do that." Papa laid the newspaper cutting flat on the table.

Gran clucked her tongue at her son. Papa glared back.

"Fwah!" said Bimble.

"Precisely!" said Mama.

Rory looked at his father. He wondered why Papa was always so angry when Gran talked about Grampa like he was still living.

Papa went back to his newspaper, a page torn from the *Farmer's Almanac*. "They're predicting more hurricanes than ever this year," he said. "If we go anywhere this summer, we'll have to be careful."

"Careful, *shmareful*," mumbled Gran.

"So we *are* going somewhere?" asked Morgan.

"I'll sleep on it tonight," said Papa, ending the conversation.

Morgan kicked Rory under the table, as if to say "I told you so," but

Rory didn't notice. His mind was swirling with questions.

Why was Gran suddenly so keen to go on an adventure?

Before bed that night, Gran went out to look for the moon, like her husband had always done. Tonight Rory followed. They leaned against Grampa's sundial and looked up at the crisp, cool crescent in the sky. Rory could hear everyone singing songs inside as they cleaned up the kitchen—except Papa, who was snapping Bimble's crib into kindling in the living room. Now was Rory's chance to tell Gran about his adventure with Glee.

"You are brave," said Gran, when Rory had finished. She looked anxiously back at the house. "Maybe in a useful way…"

"What were you and Papa talking about earlier?"

Gran turned away. "Oh, you know. Same old stuff. He'll never agree with me that Grampa could be alive out there, somewhere."

Rory was about to ask another question when Gran shuffled back to the house. She wasn't usually so secretive.

Rory raised his nose to the moon. A single bird flew silently across the ring of light. He thought of how scary it felt to be lost and alone in the bog that morning, and made a pact with himself. One day, he would find his grandfather and bring him back home.

The sun burned through the fog with ease the next morning. A sliver of light shone through a crack in the front door and fell on the twins' pillows. Morgan hopped out of the bed they shared and tore across the room to the kitchen. Rory followed behind.

"I'm making breakfast before everyone wakes up," said Morgan. He climbed onto a thread spool and grabbed the new thimble pot, lowering it onto a coiled wire burner in the hearth. Rory lit the candle underneath while Morgan scurried back and forth excitedly, grabbing a wooden spoon and throwing water, oats, and seeds into the pot. Rory poured Juneberry juice into six mugs at the table.

When Bimble woke up, she rolled out of her new feather bed and ran to the kitchen, squealing, "I grow-up mouse, now!"

"Me grow-up too!" said Morgan, teasing her. "Look at me cook!"

Bimble wrinkled her nose. "Smell funny."

Puzzled, Morgan stood over the pot. Then he suddenly ran to the table, grabbed his mug, and splashed the juice into the pot. "Much better," he said, sniffing. The porridge sputtered angrily.

"Great birds above! What is that *smell*?" Gran plopped herself down at the table as Mama hurried over to help Morgan pull the bowls down from the top shelf.

"Good morning, all," said Papa. He sat down, looking abnormally happy as he tapped a roll of paper under his arm. "Your mother and I were up late preparing something very special."

"Morgy too!" said Bimble, pointing toward the pot.

"Evidently." Papa put the roll of paper aside and resigned himself to eating.

Mama and Morgan served the porridge and sat down. Bimble immediately stuck a paw in her bowl and held up a lump. "Glue!"

Mama took the first bite. "Yum," she said. And then, "Mm. Mmm. MMMM." She motioned to Papa to pass her some juice. With a few sips, she managed to unstick her tongue from the roof of her mouth. "Maybe a little more water," she said, getting up. Everyone nodded, including Morgan, who was relieved his mother didn't choke.

"Nice going, Morg," giggled Rory. Morgan couldn't help but laugh, especially when he noticed Gran wrench apart Bimble's ears, which had been stuck together with porridge.

Mama brought the porridge back, much improved.

"Now then," said Papa, when they were all finished eating. "I have something to show you." Mama helped him unroll the paper and tack it up on the wall. Rory and Morgan's mouths dropped open. It was huge, spanning almost the entire wall.

"A map!" said Papa proudly. Gran nodded slowly in approval as Papa cleared his throat. "I've decided that today we are going on a family adventure!"

"I knew it!" said Morgan. "Hooray!" said Rory. "About time," said Gran, all at once. The twins leapt up and gave each other a paw-slap over the table, nearly knocking their mugs of juice over.

Papa frowned at his sons as he continued. "You boys had better study this map. I'll be testing you on it before we leave."

Rory and Morgan could hardly believe their luck. Their legs fidgeted under the table but they kept their paws still, careful not to do anything that would change Papa's mind.

Mama explained the map to her sons. She had painted it beautifully in watery shades of green, brown, and blue, with details in vibrant red and yellow. To the twins, it was an open window to a world of astounding possibility. Rory felt his stomach twist and groan. Would Papa really let them explore all of this?

In the bottom left corner was a little signpost that indicated the name of their home: Glasfryn. Weedle River meandered behind their tiny hill, around the bog, up the page and to the right. The fence of Biggle's farm lined the top of the riverbank, going north and stopping at a road bridge across the river. There, the fence turned right and followed the road and river east. Three miles past the farm were the towns of Eekum-Seekum, separated only by a drawbridge across the river.

Weedle River continued east, but the map stopped short. A thick black line ran from the top of the page to the bottom.

"What's that?" said Rory.

"Your father's idea of the World Beyond, I expect," said Gran dryly.

"We won't ever go that far anyway," said Papa.

"But why not?" said Rory. "Gran said our ancestors went there."

Papa's ears darkened. "Gran has told you fables. Even if a mouse could get there, he would never return to tell the tale."

"One has," mumbled Gran. She blew a crumb off her claw with a curt puff.

"Shizzle!" said Bimble, her eyes in delighted horror. "Tail gone!"

Gran shook her head at Bimble in a quick movement that meant *not now*.

Rory stared suspiciously at Gran but she wouldn't meet his eyes.

After the table was cleared and lunches were packed, the Stowaways readied themselves. Mama and Gran strapped Bimble onto Papa's back with a strip of cotton, winding it under his armpits several times, until Bimble was securely in place with a view between Papa's ears. Rory and Morgan learned how to strap their fabric pouches over one shoulder and across their bellies, so their lunches stayed put while they ran.

Papa lectured incessantly. "…And, at all costs, stay together. If you do get separated, wait at one of the designated spots and we'll find you. Do NOT talk to strangers—of any species." He finally finished, adding, "And keep watch on your grandmother. She's like a firecracker waiting to explode."

Gran rolled her eyes at Mama. "That husband of yours is one dull mouse. You'd never know he came from Grampa and me." Mama smiled as she adjusted Gran's pouch. Everyone was ready.

The Stowaways filed out the front door of Glasfryn and stood around the sundial.

"Nine o'clock," said Rory.

Gran ran her paw along the gnomon claw. "May Grampa be with us." She winked at Rory and off they went, racing down the hill.

"Wait for me!" called Morgan.

"Here we go," said Mama, smiling at Bimble. They scampered down the hill, Bimble's giggles vibrating as Papa's feet hit the ground.

ᗡᕮᕬ

Rory and Gran stopped to catch their breath at the fence around Biggle's pasture. Rory had watched the goats from high on a branch before, but had never dared go into the field. When Morgan caught up, Gran led them under the barbed wire and through the tall grass, where the goats were unable to get close enough to the fence to graze. Rory parted his way through and immediately froze. He was nose to nostril with a giant goat.

He opened his mouth to scream, but nothing came out.

"It's okay," said Gran, pushing him forward. "Goats have no interest in us."

The goat blasted a snort in Rory's face then took a bite out of the grass nearby. Rory jumped out of the way as Morgan doubled over, laughing. Rory's whiskers were dripping with beads of goat-snot.

"Think you can make friends with a goat?" said Morgan, teasing. Rory laughed and shook off his whiskers.

The pasture was a sprawling, uneven field. Dozens of goats

"May Grampa be with us."

roamed lazily between dry mud puddles and patches of grass. Baby goats chased their mothers and needled their bellies to feed. The sun warmed the smell of dung and sour milk in the air. Morgan pinched his nostrils shut, while Gran took in a deep, joyful breath.

"Ah, the smell of freedom!" She ran deftly across the field as the twins chased her tail, which sailed like a ribbon behind her.

Though Papa had always protected his sons from the farm, there was little danger there. Biggle's cat was extremely lazy, at twenty-three pounds of marmalade fur and fat. The most attention he gave a mouse was to turn his head over his great rolling neck, and spit out a squeaky *"Miat!"* The twenty or so chickens were usually absorbed around a fresh trough of corn, and the rats were too busy watching for spill to bother with any mouse. It was a peaceful, quiet place.

Gran led the way past the barn and under the opposite fence to a wooden recycling bin at the roadside, where she stopped to wait for Mama and Papa. Rory ran past her, to the open road.

"Stop!" yelled Gran.

A car whizzed past Rory's nose and he lost his balance in the blast of air. What kind of animal was that? A paw fell on his shoulder and wrenched him back.

"I *told* you not to run ahead," said Papa.

ᴼᵉ FIVE ᵉᴼ

EEKUM

After Papa explained the dangers of cars, Rory felt sick. The World was beginning to feel like a terrifying place, where any mouse would be lucky to survive.

Gran put her arm around Rory as she poked Papa in the belly. "Waiting for you was like watching a caterpillar climb a tree. We probably missed the rush into town."

Mama tugged at Papa's shoulder before he could retort. Two crows had landed in a tree across the road, the branch swaying heavily under their weight. Papa motioned to the boys to stay quiet.

Everyone hid behind the recycling bin as Gran kept watch for a ride by the road. While they waited, Morgan amused himself by making silly faces at Bimble, who tried to muffle her giggles by shoving her nose in Papa's ear. Papa was *not* amused. Rory and Morgan were about to burst out laughing when a strange rattle sounded in the distance. Disturbed, the crows flew off.

A gleaming object moved slowly toward them on the road. It

was a metal basket on wheels, with one wheel spinning aimlessly as it teetered along the gravel shoulder.

"What's that?" said Morgan. He and Rory peered around the bin.

"Our ride," said Gran.

As the cart grew near, Rory could see that it was pushed by a Human. Blue bags full of cans were piled high in the basket. A lower shelf over the wheels held a flattened cardboard box.

"Okay," said Papa. "Watch and learn: that Human is headed for town. See those bags of cans? He's collecting them to trade in for money at the recycling depot in Eekum. Line up in the grass near the gravel and when I say 'go,' jump up on that cardboard. Got it?"

Rory and Morgan nodded. Their hearts beat quickly as the rumble of the approaching cart drowned Papa's voice.

As soon as the cart reached the recycling bin, it stopped. A pair of enormous boots appeared from behind the back wheels and shuffled toward the bin, kicking up clouds of thick dust. The Stowaways lay perfectly still.

Rory looked carefully out from under his ear. He'd never been so close to a Human before. He looked old and tired, the soles nearly worn off his boots. The Human opened the recycling bin and took out all the cans, throwing them into a bag. The smell of rotting food wafted out from the bin.

"*Squawk!*"

Rory looked up. One crow had returned.

"Go!" said Papa.

Gran took off, pulling Rory and Morgan with her. Together they climbed up onto the shelf and lay between the layers of cardboard. Mama came next. The family held their breath as Papa plodded across the ground with Bimble on his back.

"*Squawk! Squawk!*" The crow landed on the road and walked quickly toward them.

"Hurry!" yelled Mama. Just as the crow lunged forward, its beak inches from Bimble, Papa leapt up and slid under the cardboard. The Human slammed the bin shut and spooked the crow, which flew off with a defiant screech.

Rory let out a breath as the Human pushed the cart forward. Maybe Papa was right—adventures *were* dangerous, even this close to home.

❧

The cart seemed to rattle along for hours, as the Human stopped at every recycling bin by the road. Rory began to feel hungry. He was about to dip inside his pouch for a snack, when he suddenly picked up the scent of something better. He stuck his nose out from under the cardboard.

Human shoes clacked loudly on the sidewalk as they rushed in and out the front door of the Fleas and Peas Market. The smell of food was overwhelming.

The Human stopped near a garbage can and the cart settled at an angle in the gutter along the street.

Papa climbed down the wheel. "To the drain!" he yelled.

Mama led everyone along the gutter to the grate. She and Rory slipped through in a flash. Morgan and Gran nearly squashed each other as they tried to get their plump bellies through the same slot at once. Papa gave them an encouraging shove then carefully climbed down with Bimble.

"Where are we?" said Rory, looking around. They were in a smooth, concrete tunnel below street level. A stream of water trickled past their feet.

"In a rainwater drain," said Mama. She squeezed Rory's paw and led him down the tunnel. "Wait till you see this."

The Stowaways traveled in single file around a corner, toward the back of the market.

"In my day, we were brave enough to go through the front door!" grumbled Gran.

"We're not going to the market," said Mama. "We're going underneath." She pointed to a narrow crack in the wall and began to unravel Bimble from Papa's back so he could fit through.

The aroma of delicious food wafted from the crack. Gran sniffed the air curiously but Rory and Morgan couldn't wait.

"Stop!" cried Papa, as they disappeared through the hole.

At the end of the passage, the twins stopped, amazed. They looked out over a huge room, only ten inches tall but as wide as Biggle's field and lit by a grid of Christmas lights that hung from the ceiling.

Town mice dressed in aprons and waistcoats roamed between rows of tiny market stalls below. Little mice in overalls chased each other up the aisles, squealing with delight at pyramids of fresh berries. Some grabbed the berries from the bottom rows with their naughty paws and sent the piles rolling across the floor.

Net sacks filled with nuts, marshmallows, fruit gummies, puffed rice, and spicy potato rings hung from the rafters. There were pots of honey and jam as big as their heads, bars of soap gnawed into heart shapes, buckets of buttercups, bales of bedding feathers bound with ribbon, bedposts, rocking chairs, tables, pots, pans, dishes, and mirrors—all perfectly crafted in mouse-scale.

"A feast!" cried Morgan, jumping to the floor. Rory helped Gran down while Mama lifted Bimble onto Papa's back again.

"Wanna stay down!" cried Bimble, squirming. Two young mice sped by, one pulling the other's tail as he yelled for his chocolate chip back. "*Bad* mice," whispered Bimble, and she held tight again.

"Okay!" said Papa, eyeing Morgan, who was about to run off. "We'll stay in groups and meet back here at one o'clock." He pointed to a stall hung with watch faces. Morgan dashed down an aisle that smelled particularly tasty. Papa ran after him.

Mama, Rory and Gran weaved slowly through the crowd, taking in the sights. Most town mice barely noticed them but others pointed and sniggered at the "naked country bumpkins" with the "weird monkey tails."

"Hmpf," said Gran. "I'd like to see them scavenge in the woods in those outfits! And really, is *any* of this necessary?" she said, dismissing the whole market with her paw. But when they passed by a stall with tiny, fresh croissants, she suddenly lowered her voice. "How do we get one of those? Do we just ask for it?"

"No," said Mama. "It's a barter system. You have to trade."

"With what?" said Gran, bewildered.

Mama smiled. "I packed something in your pouches."

Rory rustled through the thistle seeds in his pouch and found a little box, cut and folded neatly, made from an old milk carton. He took it out and sniffed. It was Juneberry paste—a rare delicacy to town mice, who would never dare go in the woods to harvest berries themselves.

"Your father doesn't know I made them," said Mama. "But I thought it would be fun to trade." Papa and Morgan were ahead several stalls down the aisle. Mama hurried over to explain the trading-boxes to Papa. He looked sceptical, but before he could protest, Morgan was off like a shot with his box in his paw. Papa followed him with a sigh.

Gran and Rory caught up with Mama, who had stopped at a stall selling housewares.

"Juneberry paste, you say?" said the vendor to Mama. "Yep, I'll take it. Have a look around and let me know what you like. We take money, too."

"Human money?" said Mama, surprised.

"Nope. Mouse money. Up in Grule, we call them pinheads." The vendor pulled a metal coin out of his waistcoat pocket then slid it back quickly. Mama nodded distantly while she explored the items on the table.

Gran inspected the tines of a wonky wire fork. "Our claws are better than *this*," she said loudly. She plunked it back on the table and tugged Rory down the aisle.

"Gran, where's Grule?" asked Rory.

"In the World Beyond."

"That mouse was from the *World Beyond*?" said Rory, dumbfounded. He looked back at the vendor, who continued to chat with Mama.

"Not much use, is he?" said Gran, snorting.

Rory's mind raced. "I thought the World Beyond was far away," he said.

"It is, but not so far that our ancestors didn't travel there—I told you stories about them."

"Yeah, but I thought it was *really* far away. I mean, farther than we could ever go."

"Your father seems to think so," said Gran. The look of frustration on her face suddenly erupted into a grin. She stopped in front of a stall where a vendor was demonstrating his range of cat-teasers. He poked the pad of a fake cat foot with a feather duster as he explained how the new extendable handle made it safer to tickle cats from a longer distance. Gran laughed so hard she almost cried, while throngs of curious mice pushed in front of Rory to see what was going on.

Rory backed away from the crowd and wandered down the aisle alone. What was so bad about the World Beyond that kept Papa from traveling there? Wouldn't anybody tell him? He saw a stall piled high with books—so high that the vendor's nose was only visible through a small opening. Rory had never seen a whole book before, and certainly not for mice. Maybe one of them was written about the World Beyond. He stepped a little closer.

Each book had a colored cardboard cover with a beautiful cloth spine. One in particular looked intriguing. In delicate gold lettering, the spine read: *Ten Easy Ways Out of Common Scrapes*. Rory carefully wiggled the book out of the stack, which wobbled precariously. He could feel the vendor's stare as he put his nose down and leafed through the pages.

> Obviously, birds are not our friends. They are ferocious, selfish animals, whose only use for you is to feed their screeching babies and line their nests with your fine fur coat. Should you ever have the misfortune of crossing the path of a feathered freak, here are the ten best ways to escape impending doom:

1. ***Carry a cocktail umbrella***. When you hear a bird overhead, simply open the paper umbrella, crouch down underneath, and appear to be a piece of human litter lying in the path.

2. ***Wear perfume***. Sprinkle yourself with lavender water to confuse their sense of smell (The perfume and umbrella together will also be an asset to your style).

3. ***Don't go out at night***. Eat in. Order takeout. Let the delivery mice risk their lives…

Rory's mind wandered off the page as he tried to make sense of it all. Mr. Glee wasn't ferocious…and what was a "delivery mouse"? It seemed like everyone was trying to make him afraid of everything. But was the World really so scary?

"Got any books on mousetraps?" A large mouse in a shiny jacket approached the book vendor. "I got a great big live one outside my hole. Gotta deactivate it before my aunt comes up from Grule."

"Of course, sir. Let's see…" The vendor disappeared behind the stack of books.

The shiny mouse looked down at Rory and nodded. "Hello! Whatcha readin'?"

Rory opened his mouth to reply but before he could answer, the vendor reappeared. "Here you are," he said. "This one explains how to disable even the most complicated trap."

"How many pinheads?"

"Three, sir."

The shiny mouse dropped the coins into the vendor's paw. "Thanks, pal. Now my aunt won't suffer the fate of that old country mouse—you know, like the one in that book of fables you sold me. My young ones never tire of that story!" As he moved off, he gave Rory a wink. "Chin up, chum—you'll look taller! Ha ha ha!" He disappeared into the crowd.

Rory moved in front of the vendor's window, where he stood on the tips of his claws.

"What book was that mouse talking about, sir?" Rory spoke loudly over the din of the market.

"You like fables, son? I have a copy here somewhere." The vendor disappeared behind the stack again and popped up with a tiny book in his paw, half the size of the others. "There are some classics in this one. But I believe the story you're asking about is a newer one, added to the latest edition. Yes, it's here. 'The Proud Mouse and the Trap,' about an old mouse who thought he could outsmart anything—some strange breed from the country."

Rory felt a shiver go up his spine. The noise of the market grew dim around him as little bells seemed to ring in his ears. A proud country mouse…a strange breed…a trap… Was this story about *Grampa*?

"I can trade you." Rory threw down the book he was reading and rummaged through his pouch. He gave the little box to the vendor.

"Juneberries?" said the vendor, sniffing greedily at the paste. He passed the book of fables to Rory, who snatched it quickly and ran back up the aisle.

Gran walked on her hind feet down the aisle, using her brand new extendable cat-tickler like a walking stick. Its feathers vibrated like a plumed tree above her as it hit the ground with each of her steps. She felt majestic, like an exotic queen wielding her ruling staff—

The clock suddenly struck one. Bells and whistles and chimes and cuckoos all sounded off together. Gran jumped high in fright and bumped her head on a rafter. The tickler flew out of her paw toward several mice who squealed and ran away. Gran fell down with a crash and rolled under the clock seller's table. A moment passed before she felt someone hover over her.

"Wake up!"

"Willis!"

"No, Gran, it's me—Rory!" He shook her gently.

"Will, please...come back! Nooooo!"

Rory shook her again. "Gran! Wake up!"

The clock seller appeared at Rory's side and stood over him. "Here. Get her to smell this." He gave Rory a box of chili powder, and Rory held it under Gran's nose. She immediately sneezed and sat up, bumping her head on the table.

"Ouch! Great gobs of bird dung! Where am I?"

"At the market." Rory retrieved the tickler, which Gran leaned on heavily to get up.

"Ah, yes—the market," she said. "Where mice dress up like fools." She turned her nose up at the clock seller's fancy waistcoat. "Come on, Rory. Let's go."

"You were really out of it, Gran. You thought I was Grampa!"

"Nonsense, you're obviously too short."

"You kept calling his name and yelling at him to come back."

"Hmpf." Gran put her paw on Rory's shoulder. "Let's go find your father—it's one o'clock."

Bimble was holding a lollipop as big as her head when Rory and Gran caught up with the family at the hole in the wall.

"I pick a pop!" said Bimble. "Whad'joo pick?"

Gran tickled Bimble's ears with the feather duster while Rory patted his pouch. "I found a book I wanted," he said quietly. Gran gave him an inquisitive look.

"I got this cool game, Ror," said Morgan. "Look!"

Rory looked over his brother's shoulder. The shallow wooden box had a maze of walls inside, under a clear plastic top. Morgan angled the box up and down as three little balls rolled inside. "It's called the Amazer. See, you have to get the green balls in the hole at the end of the maze without letting the red ball fall through the trap in the middle."

"Oh, put it away," said Papa. He turned to Gran. "And what is that thing? No doubt some sort of peace-disturber." He eyed the cat-tickler.

"What put a kink in your tail?" Gran retracted the handle and slid it under her pouch strap.

"He's upset because I condoned trade with town mice," said Mama with a smile.

"Score!" Morgan yelled as he got one of the green balls into the hole.

"What did you get?" Gran asked Mama.

"Bimble and I went for the tasty pastries." Mama held out her pouch, which was stuffed with baked goods. "We'll have a picnic somewhere. And since your son doesn't approve of trading, he can eat thistle seed instead!"

Papa frowned.

"Double score!" Morgan sunk the second ball.

"Oh stop your games, all of you!" said Papa. "And get Bimble off me so we can go back through the crack." He took the lollipop from Bimble and bent down so Mama could undo her bindings.

"Pip took my *pop* away!" cried Bimble.

"Papa's taken all of our pop away," said Gran. Rory watched the smile drift off her face, replaced by a look of worry. Something was *definitely* not right.

FABLES AND FOES

The Stowaways enjoyed a lazy picnic under an azalea in Eekum Park, and then made their way through the street drains out to the main road, where they waited for a ride back to Biggle's farm. It wasn't long before a bulldozer crawler appeared, creeping slowly along the shoulder of the road to allow cars to pass. It was easy to jump on at that pace.

Papa, Gran, and Mama sat on a bar between the front and back wheels while Rory and Morgan jumped onto the inside of the crawler track, which rotated slowly around the wheels. They held on like monkeys, joyfully dangling as it went round and round like a Ferris wheel.

"Careful you don't get pinched in the treads where it turns!" yelled Papa over the rumble of the bulldozer.

"This is a pleasant ride," said Mama, settling down comfortably.

"Willis and I used to ride on these machines." Gran smiled to herself. "When the Humans rebuilt Eekum Park, bulldozers traveled constantly up and down this road. Long ago, now."

"Why did they rebuild the park?" asked Mama.

"A hurricane blew all the trees down and caused a terrible mess."

"Oh, that sounds scary!"

"Ah well, Weedle Mice always survive, don't we? Just like ol' Grampa." Gran stroked Bimble's cheek as she slept on Papa's back. Papa shot Gran a grouchy look.

Rory and Morgan let their tails skim over Papa's ears as the crawler moved overhead. "Oh, get off!" said Papa, swatting at them like flies. They giggled as the crawler moved forward, taking them out of reach.

"So what did you trade for at the market?" Mama asked Papa.

"I won't trade with town mice."

"Why not?" she said, smiling.

"They don't respect us. You heard them call us names."

"You happily ate one of their iced buns an hour ago."

Papa dropped his voice to a whisper as the boys went by on the crawler below. "Town mice have adopted evils from the World Beyond. We must be careful—look what happened to my father."

"Humans are responsible for Grampa's loss, not mice!" said Mama.

"Shh!" said Papa. Rory turned the corner toward him.

Gran scowled. "We should have searched while in town."

"There's nothing to *search* for, Mother," said Papa.

Mama patted Gran's paw. "We don't know where to look yet. Be patient."

"What are you looking for?" Rory asked, directly overhead now. But the crawler carried him away again before anyone could answer.

When the recycling bin at Biggle's farm came into view, the Stowaways lined up on the bar and jumped down. They scurried across the road, through the ditch, under the fence, and around the corner of the barn. The rumble of the bulldozer faded in the distance.

Biggle's field was peaceful after the hubbub of town. The afternoon sun had lowered in the sky and the goats were napping in the shadow of a lone maple tree. The only sound was the babble of human children racing toy boats in the pond. The Stowaways ambled across the pasture as Mama led them in single file down a narrow path.

"What you got there, Granny?" a gruff voice called out, laughing. It was Harry Belter, sunbathing on a tuft of grass with his sons, Wally and Dill. "You bring your feather bed with you everywhere? Well, I guess an ancient mouse like you could fall asleep anytime!"

Gran whipped out the cat-tickler and extended the pole. "Maybe I should show you how it works!" Ignoring Harry's insult, Papa pushed his mother along.

Wally laughed hysterically until he noticed Morgan and Rory coming down the path. "That's the mouse who cut my fur!" he said, elbowing Dill.

Morgan stopped suddenly, grinning with delight at the sight of Wally's patchy head. "*You* did that, Ror?"

"Shh!" said Rory. He sped up and ran past Morgan, who scampered after him down the path.

"Your day's coming, weaklings!" Wally jeered. "Mark my words!"

At the opposite side of the pasture, the Stowaways heard a noise coming from the other side of the fence. Gran stuck her head through the grass to investigate.

"Oh! You gave me a fright!" Miss Creemore dropped the doormat she had been banging against the fence post. Dust billowed out in clouds all around her. "Good thing I've seen you—I've decided to have the Annual Weedle Mouse Meeting during the Student Frolic tomorrow."

"We'll be there," said Mama. "Why not come over later for a visit, though? We should probably talk about...uh, you know—" Mama stopped herself as Papa shook his head at her.

Morgan rolled his eyes. After all the trouble he had caused at school, a visit from the teacher was the last thing he wanted. But Rory looked intently at his parents. What were they being so secretive about?

"Good idea," said Miss Creemore, looking down at Morgan. "There are things we should discuss." She picked up the doormat and continued to beat it against the fencepost.

The Stowaways rambled lazily down the bank and along the old streambed. Morgan babbled about all the toys he had seen at the market while Rory responded with distant grunts of interest, his mind firmly set on the book of fables and when he might get a chance to read it. Bimble slept soundly on Papa's back as Gran described the various cat-teasers she had seen that morning. Mama giggled and even Papa blurted out a chuckle when she imitated a bewildered cat, driven mad by the tickler.

When the Stowaways reached the final leg of the path up to Glasfryn, the boys cheered, "Home!" and everyone ran up the hill, eager to take off their pouches and relax before dinner. But when they reached their front garden, they were met with a shock.

The sundial was toppled over and lay on the ground. A disturbing expression had been drawn on its face in thick, chalky slashes. The gnomon claw looked like a nose between a toothy snarl and angry eyes. The Stowaways stood in silence, their spirits crumbled.

Their beloved monument to Grampa was ruined.

Gran finally ran to the sundial and tried to pick it up. Rory moved to help her but Papa had already run past him to help his mother haul the rock upright again. Mama rushed over and rubbed at the chalk with the fur on her elbow, but it only smudged into a cloudy mess. She sent Morgan inside for a bucket of water and some scrub brushes, and then she unbound Bimble and put her to bed. Papa followed them inside and lit a fire in the hearth, where he sat quietly and stared at the flames.

The sun dipped low over the river. The orange light glimmered through the tip of the gnomon claw as Rory and Morgan helped Gran scrub the sundial. When the light was nearly gone, Morgan quit and went inside. Rory stayed with Gran, who continued to scrub, her ears drawn back in determination as she pushed a brush back and forth over an angry chalk eyebrow. Her face looked as hard as the stone.

Miss Creemore knocked on the door of Glasfryn with four quick raps. A breeze stirred over Weedle River and gently rustled the flowers she held in her paw. It was dark outside but the Stowaways' home, with its white clay walls, glowed dully in the moonlight.

When no one answered, Miss Creemore leaned back. Through the buttercups that grew over the kitchen window, she could see the curtains were drawn. But curls of wispy smoke drifted down from the chimneys. *Some*one must be home. She put her ear to the door and knocked again, louder. Finally she heard the sound of pattering feet across the floor.

Rory opened the door with a candle in his paw.

"We're all in the kitchen, except Bimble and Gran," he whispered. He nodded toward the far corner of the living room by the fireplace, where Gran was nestled in her sack of feathers, a blanket pulled up over her face. Bimble slept silently in her new bed nearby.

"I see." Miss Creemore gently closed the door behind her and followed Rory to the kitchen. Papa and Mama were putting away the dinner dishes while Morgan sat at the table, absorbed with the Amazer.

"These are for you." Miss Creemore gave the flowers to Mama and greeted Papa with a smile.

Papa put a pot of water on the burner in the hearth. "Blueberry tea?"

"Yes, thanks," said Miss Creemore.

"Thank you for these—they're a welcome sight to us all this evening." Mama arranged the flowers in a vase.

Miss Creemore's ears perked up. "Oh? What's happened?"

"Someone ruined our sundial."

"Oh, dear!"

"Gran took it really hard. That sundial means so much to her, and with everything else that happened this week…" Mama wiped a tear from her eye. "I don't suppose there's any change on that front, is there?"

"No, dear, nothing new to report," said Miss Creemore.

Rory looked at his teacher suspiciously. "What else happened this week?" he asked. But Miss Creemore only squeezed his paw.

Rory turned to Papa instead. "What *else* happened this week?"

"We just don't know who would want to ruin our sundial," said Papa quickly, ignoring Rory.

"We'll address it at the meeting tomorrow," said Miss Creemore.

"You know how other Weedle Mice feel about us," said Mama. "We don't want to make things worse by accusing anyone of vandalism."

Papa brought the teapot to the table with three mugs. "We have to face this. We can't ignore their insults anymore."

"He's right, dear," said Miss Creemore. "We've got to stop this conflict. Even yesterday at school, Morgan and Rory were arguing with Wally again." Rory looked down at the floor while Morgan continued to play with the Amazer, unaware his name had been mentioned.

Papa opened his mouth to say something but Mama spoke first. "It won't happen again," she said before Papa could scold the twins. "So, how should we broach the subject at the meeting tomorrow?"

Papa took the pot of boiling water off the flame and poured some into the teapot with dried blueberries. He let it steep as he, Mama and Miss Creemore quietly talked.

Rory grew tired of watching Morgan play with the Amazer. His mind wandered to the book of fables he'd bought at the market. He slid off the end of the bench and tiptoed quietly back to the living room, where he took his pouch off his hook by the door. He was eager to read the book alone.

He settled into the big comfy chair by the fireplace. He was glad their home wasn't damaged too. Grampa had built it long ago and named it Glasfryn, an ancient word meaning "the sound of running water." Rory listened to the river outside as he let his fur mesh with the velvet chair and his feet sink into the moss rug. He felt surrounded by his grandfather, as if the old mouse was actually there in the room with his grandson.

A twig snapped in the fire and a spark flew up in the air, lighting Gran's ears on her pillow before it fell into ash. Rory quickly opened his pouch and pulled out the book. He pawed the silver lettering down the red cloth spine: *Fables To Live By, Collected and Adapted in Grule by Malika Onion-Fair.*

Rory opened the book to the first page and found the table of contents. He scanned down until he found the title he wanted. There it was, at the bottom; "The Proud Mouse and the Trap." He flipped the pages to the last story and began to read:

> There was a proud old mouse from the country who often went to town to brag about himself. One day, he stood on the steps outside the Museum of Zoology, twirled his long tail and boasted to all the mice who went by that he was better at anything they could do, even at his age.
>
> The town mice yelled back, "You're crazy!" and there was such a commotion of squeaks that even the Humans began to notice them before they all scurried away into the bushes.
>
> The next day, the proud mouse went back again and found a mousetrap on the stair. It was a mesh wire box with a piece of cheese at one end and a trap door poised above the opening. The old mouse boasted to a group of town mice that he could get the cheese out of the trap before the door

closed, because he could do anything better than
they could.

The town mice said, "If you must prove you are faster
and smarter and better than us, please do."

The proud mouse ran inside the trap and the door
immediately closed. A Human came out of the museum and picked up the trap.

"You *are* an extraordinary mouse, aren't you?" said
the Human, and took him away.

Moral:

Mice who boast create their own demise.

Rory's ears drooped as he put the book down. He had hoped the
story was about Grampa, since the bookseller said it was about a
strange breed of country mouse. But there was no mention of the
Stowaway name or even the Weedle Mice breed, apart from the
long tail. And he'd never heard the word *zoology* before, though
Gran did once talk about a museum in Seekum.

Rory picked up the book and read it again, and then a third
time. But he still couldn't make it mean anything. He had hoped it
would lead to Grampa. He wanted to make Gran happy again.

Rory looked over at her. The blanket had slid off her face and her
mouth was half open. She wheezed as her breath hissed across the

pillow. Should he tell her about the fable, or would she think him silly for thinking it could help them find Grampa?

"Time for bed." Papa tweaked Rory's ear gently as Mama and Miss Creemore said goodnight at the door. Morgan flopped on their bed and stretched out his limbs, covering more than half of it. Rory sighed and put the book down.

"So this is what you got today?" Papa picked it up to examine it. "It's quite impressive, a mouse-sized book. I guess these city mice are skilled, if nothing else."

Mama came up beside him and took the book from his paw. "It's a wondrous thing to be able to read, especially something so beautiful." She flipped the pages and they fluttered to a halt. "'The Proud Mouse and the Trap'—that looks like an interesting story." She closed the book and gave it back to Rory with a nose-rub, then returned to the kitchen with Papa.

Rory moved to his side of the bed and slid the book underneath the sack of feathers. He climbed up and yanked hard on the blanket for his share, but Morgan was already asleep like a dead weight on top of it. Rory gave up and slept at the edge of the bed, partially covered. After a while he dozed off, the soft voices of his parents lulling him to sleep.

"I'm concerned about Rory," whispered Mama, watching her son from the kitchen. "He seems preoccupied lately."

"He's always been a worrier," said Papa quietly.

"Yes, but this time it's different. You don't think he knows anything, do you?"

"No—how could he?"

"Gran might have told him."

Papa paused. "Even she wouldn't take that risk. The boys are too young yet."

❧

Rory sat up, his heart pounding. He was backed into the corner of a cage as a giant eye peered down at him. "You're an extraordinary *mouse," boomed a human voice, laughing.*

The light went out in the kitchen and Rory heard his parents cross the floor toward their bed. He sighed in relief; it was only a dream.

SEVEN

THE FROLIC

A damp chill hovered over the bog surrounding Glasfryn. Rory wiped a layer of dew off the sundial and shuddered, vaguely recalling his nightmare. He adjusted the scarf around his neck as Gran stepped outside, wrapped in a blanket.

"Mornin'," said Rory.

Gran didn't respond as she trudged toward the sundial and ran her paw over the scar that remained on its face.

"I read a story from that book I got," said Rory, trying to distract her.

Gran lifted her ears slightly. "Oh?"

"It's about a mouse who gets caught in a trap…"

"Sounds depressing." Her ears fell.

"Well, it's a fable—it's supposed to teach a lesson, I guess." Rory wished he hadn't mentioned it.

"Surely you already know to avoid *traps*." Gran pulled the blanket tighter and shuffled back to the house. Rory followed sadly.

Everyone was eating breakfast in the kitchen, except Morgan, who'd already finished and was hunched over the Amazer again.

As Rory joined them, Morgan looked up. "Hey, that's mine!" He yanked the scarf around his brother's neck.

"Ow! Watch it! You're choking me."

"Don't steal my stuff, then."

"Well *you* took the whole blanket last night," said Rory.

"We're supposed to share in this house," warned Mama.

"Yeah! Brudders share!" Bimble made a picture of an angry face with the seeds on her plate.

Morgan ignored the reprimands. "When we go back to town next week, I'm going to get the 3-D Amazer. It's so cool! It's a cube with connecting mazes on every side. Do we have more Juneberry paste to trade?" he asked, without looking up.

"I think next time we should go somewhere else," said Mama.

Papa nodded. "Sounds good to me."

"Well, you can count me out," said Gran. "You'll never go where *I* want to go."

"But it won't be a family adventure if you don't come," said Rory. He nudged Morgan. "Right?"

Morgan didn't seem to hear.

"I'm too old for all this." Gran stood up.

"But you'll come to the meeting, right?" asked Mama. "The boys can take care of Bimble at the frolic."

"If I must. But if Harry insults me again, I may not be as polite as usual!" Gran thrashed her tail in the air and marched off to the living room.

Mama winked at Rory. "She'll be fine, you'll see. If the meeting doesn't light her up like dynamite, *then* we can worry."

Weedle Mice meetings always took place at the school. Miss Creemore stacked the desks out of the way and rolled the benches toward the front of the room, leaving standing room at the back for extra mice.

Weedle Mice began to trickle in. Mr. Noseworthy, who would co-chair the meeting with Miss Creemore, arrived first. Harry and Callie Belter, Wally and Dill's parents, sat in the back row. Mack and Jack, the orphans who lived on a toy boat in the bog, took a bench near the refreshments table. Callie pinched her nose to block the smell of their unwashed fur.

When the Stowaways entered, the crowd went quiet. Papa, Gran, and Mama took a bench in the middle of the room.

"Well," said Gran, noticing the hush. "What are you all looking at?" Papa sat his mother down as the crowd returned to normal volume.

Soon it was standing room only. As a few tardy mice hurried in, Mr. Noseworthy's whiskers twitched nervously. It was time to begin.

Miss Creemore stood up and banged on the desk with her gavel. "Fellow Weedle mice," she said as a hundred eyes fell on her. "Thank you all for coming. Mr. Noseworthy will quickly review last year's notes before we discuss new matters. Let's be courteous and let others finish before we speak, all right? Mr. Noseworthy, your floor." She sat down.

Mr. Noseworthy stood as tall as he could, coughing weakly. "Ahem. Thank you, Miss Creemore. Delighted to be here. Let's see, er...item number one..."

Several mice rolled their eyes and others shifted their legs uncomfortably as Mr. Noseworthy droned on through more than twenty items.

❧

After saying goodbye to Mama at the school, Rory and Morgan led Bimble to a clearing among the trees, where the Student Frolic took place at the end of every school year. The rest of the students were already gathered on the oval activity track. Bimble held Morgan's paw, wide-eyed.

"You're going to be a breeze at Ring-nut," said Morgan, squeezing her paw.

"Whutsa wing-nut?" said Bimble, eyeing Mrs. Noseworthy, Mr. Noseworthy's robust wife.

"Attention!" screamed Mrs. Noseworthy. Her eyes bulged out of her head as she whistled between her claws. "Young ones go with Miss Wye to learn Ring-nut and older students stay with me on the track. We're playing Baneberry Pass. Pair up!"

Miss Wye collected Bimble and the other young mice and took them to a sandpit inside the oval. Rory and Morgan moved into the crowd on the track.

Mrs. Noseworthy counted up the older group. There were an even ten, but Dill wasn't supposed to be there since he was no longer in school.

"Dill, I'll let you stay, but you're too big to team up with Wally. You'll each have to pair up with one of my daughters, Tamrin and Rayna. It's only fair to the smaller mice."

Tamrin and Rayna smiled insincerely at Wally and Dill.

"Spoiled rotten," sulked Wally.

"We can win this now!" said Morgan, excited to see Wally and Dill split up. "You do the second lap, Ror. You're faster."

"Listen up!" said Mrs. Noseworthy. "The object is to sprint around the track, holding a berry with your tail. At the second lap you stop and relay it to your partner's tail, without using your paws. If you drop the berry, you're out. Take your places!"

Mrs. Noseworthy gave a berry to Morgan. He wound it tightly in his tail and hunched down at the start line. Tamrin and Rayna, who would take the first laps for their teams, readied themselves in a lane on either side of Morgan. The other mice took their lanes.

"Readeeee—GO!" shouted Mrs. Noseworthy.

Morgan kicked off as fast as he could, expecting the girls to fall behind, but the smaller mice were right on his heels. As the lanes merged at the first bend, Tamrin moved slightly ahead, elbowing him as she passed. Rayna stuck her paw out and grabbed Morgan's hind leg. He fell instantly, tripping the other mice behind him. Tamrin and Rayna roared into the lead.

Back at the start line, Wally and Dill leaned on each other in fits of laughter. "What a loser," snorted Wally.

Rory ignored them as he peered anxiously down the track. The other fallen mice stood up sadly, with their berries in their paws. Morgan jumped up, his berry still firmly in his tail.

"Yesss!" shouted Rory. "Hurry, Morg!"

Tamrin and Rayna roared into the lead.

Morgan tore down the track, but the girls had already reached the start line as he rounded the final bend. Tamrin and Wally struggled desperately to relay the berry and their tails tangled in a knot. Rayna and Dill quietly focused, and within seconds they made the exchange. Dill was off like a shot, just as a gasping Morgan finally reached the start line.

"Lie down with your tail on your belly!" said Rory. Morgan flopped on the ground gladly. Tamrin and Wally finally finished their exchange just before Rory scooped the berry out of Morgan's tail with his own. Wally pushed off the start line, flicking divots of dirt in Rory's face.

Rory threw his ears back and ran after him. Wally was on the inside track and moving fast, but Rory was much faster. As he passed him at the first bend, his tail whipped hard against Wally's cheek. A cloud of dust flew up as Wally faltered.

"If you drop that berry you're *out*, Stowaway!" yelled Mrs. Noseworthy. But neither berry fell.

"Go, Ror, go!" Morgan threw his fist in the air, accidentally punching Tamrin in the nose. Tamrin pushed him down on the track and before Dill could reach the finish line, he tripped over Morgan. The other mice yelled at the commotion as Dill took a swing at Morgan.

Rory sped up and leapt onto Dill, forcing him to the ground before he could hit Morgan. Morgan tried to hold Rory back, but when Wally crossed the finish line he immediately aimed for Morgan.

The students cheered at the brawl on the ground. "Wal-ly! Wal-ly! Wal-ly!"

Mrs. Noseworthy whistled wildly but no one paid attention. Miss Wye ran over to help stop the fight, and the two adults grabbed Wally and Dill by the scruff of their necks. Rory and Morgan stumbled to their feet.

"Morgan ruined the race!" cried Tamrin.

"I did not," said Morgan, his nostrils flaring. "You pushed me on the track, you stinker!"

"I don't stink—your whole family stinks!"

"My family is the smartest in Weedle River! And my brother is the bravest."

"Oh yeah?"

"Yeah! He even talks to birds!"

"Morgan, *nooo*...!" Rory put his paws over his eyes.

᷍᷍

"...And that is the last straw...er...item from the agenda." Mr. Noseworthy stumbled to a halt, let out a breath, and looked up anxiously. Though there had been much grumbling throughout his review, everyone was silent.

"Good," said Miss Creemore, moving to the blackboard. "If there are no further comments on last meeting's issues, we can make a new agenda. Mr. Noseworthy, please direct us."

"Er, will anyone suggest a first topic?" asked Mr. Noseworthy. Various mice looked about the room.

"Yes," called out Papa. "Our sundial was vandalized."

Miss Creemore wrote it on the board: *#1: Vandalism.*

"Serves them right!" yelled out Callie Belter.

"Any other issues?" said Mr. Noseworthy, looking hopefully at the crowd.

"What else is there to talk about? The Stowaways are a menace to us all," said Callie. "One of their boys ruined my son's fur!" Murmurs swelled among the crowd.

"*No* other topics?" Mr. Noseworthy tapped the desk with his pencil.

A small voice from one side of the room spoke up. "Well, my arthritis is getting worse and it would be nice if some young mice could help me."

"Ah, Miss Dafne. Thank you. Shall we name your topic Helping the Elderly?" Mr. Noseworthy smiled with relief, then added quickly, "If there are no more suggestions, we'll begin our discussion with that."

Miss Creemore glared down at him. "Should we not discuss item number *one* first, Mr. Noseworthy?"

"Get the Stowaways to help the elderly! Those pack rats have more stuff then anyone—they should give it to the old mice!"

"Noted. Spoken by Mrs. Quenell." Mr. Noseworthy wrote it down.

"Fine for you to say, nut-hoarder!" said Miss Bucket, sitting next to Mama. Beryl-Ann Bucket was a rare friend to the Stowaways.

Miss Creemore stood over Mr. Noseworthy. "We really must deal with the issues that have been unearthed by this vandalism, do you not agree, Mr. Noseworthy?"

"Er…fine then." He put down his pencil. "Mr. Stowaway, would you like to say something about your sundial?"

"We'd like to know why someone wrecked it," said Papa.

"What do Weedle Mice need to know the time for, anyway?" Mack bellowed out through a mouthful of berries. "Sun comes up, sun goes down. In between, we eat."

"Keeping time is for townies!" shouted Jack.

"We live as we choose and you live as you choose. We don't judge your lifestyle," said Papa.

"Well at least we keep to ourselves," said Jack.

"Hard not to, when you live on a boat, mate!" Someone snickered from the crowd.

"We also keep to ourselves," said Mama. She held her foot over Gran's tail, which was impatiently drumming the floor.

"Oh no, you don't. You mingle with town mice," Callie snarled.

Other mice stood up around the room and joined in. "One of these days they'll bring townies back here!"

"They'll be swarming our fields and taking our food!"

"We'll end up as half-breeds!"

Most of the mice were up on their feet now. "That sundial probably came from a townie!"

Papa stood. "My mother made that sundial and it's our property. Whoever vandalized it is the criminal here, not us!"

Harry Belter stood up slowly. "Well, if you didn't get around so much we wouldn't have to keep you in your place."

"Is that a confession?" said Papa. Gran jumped up, ready to pounce.

"Where's your feather duster, Granny?" jeered Harry.

"That's it, Belter, you've had your last word!" Gran lashed her tail in the air. It soared over Papa's head and nearly slashed Harry's cheek.

"Here we go!" Some of the mice turned around in their seats for a better view.

Mr. Noseworthy dropped his pencil on the floor and bent down, pretending to look for it.

"ENOUGH!" said Miss Creemore. "I am appalled at the lack of solidarity in this room. A family of Weedle Mice has been brutally insulted and you choose to argue rather than help." Her ears bent back as she looked for Mr. Noseworthy, who was nowhere to be seen. "Oh, get up!" She banged her gavel hard on the desk and Mr. Noseworthy popped up, holding the pencil as if he had finally found it. Miss Creemore sighed. "Anyone who wants to speak must come to the front. Everyone else *be quiet*."

Papa encouraged Gran to sit back down on the bench where Mama held her down. He moved to the front of the room and stood to face the crowd.

"Fellow Weedle Mice." He cleared his throat. "Our family explores our surroundings only for the love of knowledge. We are as committed to préserving our territory as you are. In good faith, let us offer to keep watch outside our borders, reporting back to all of you on the status of our security."

"How do you know the townies haven't followed you home already?" said Harry. "It was probably one of them who attacked your sundial—and soon they'll attack all of us!"

A chorus of whispers swept over the room.

"You wouldn't know a townie if you met one, you daft slug!" yelled out Gran. Papa cringed while Mama shushed her.

Harry continued. "The Stowaways might already be friends with townies. And what about that falcon's claw on their sundial? I bet they're friends with birds too!"

"How do you know about the talon, Harry? You've never been to our house." The fur rose on Papa's head.

"Umm...your sons must've mentioned it to Wally at school...." Harry looked away.

"I doubt that very much," said Papa, clenching his fists.

Just then, Tamrin and Rayna burst into the room and ran up the aisle toward Mr. Noseworthy. "Daddy, Daddy! Guess what? Rory Stowaway talks to *birds*!"

Rory stumbled in after the girls but stopped short near the door. Every mouse was glaring at him. Except Gran, who buried her face in her paws.

A Secret Revealed

Heat rose off the sundial in the midday sun, distorting Rory's view with ascending rivulets of hot air. He lay on Gran's lounge chair, thinking bleakly of what had happened over the past week.

Papa had barely spoken to him since the Annual Meeting. He was furious with Gran for not telling him that Rory had befriended a bird, and equally disappointed in Rory for starting a fight at the frolic—information that Bimble let slip and Morgan happily outlined in detail. Gran vowed never to go on family adventures again, since Papa was "as dull as dishwater," and spent every minute she could picking Juneberries, which piled into a mountain in the yard.

Mama had tried to restore the peace by suggesting they build their own Ring-nut pit, but only Morgan and Bimble were excited by the idea. Together they dug a sandpit and fixed a hazelnut on a bouncy spring in the middle. They played the game endlessly, tossing washer rings over the bouncing nut—much to the annoyance of Papa, who sometimes caught a stray ring on his ear as he scowled in his lounge chair.

But worst of all, Rory had been grounded all week and couldn't leave their hill.

"I'm going to the field!" Morgan burst out of the house.

Rory sat up. "Says who?"

"Papa's letting me scavenge with them today!"

A dragonfly flew low over Rory's face, its wings buzzing loudly. Irritated, he shook his ears.

"What's your problem?" said Morgan.

"Well, in case you haven't noticed, you let it slip at the frolic that I made friends with a bird, and now our family is ruined."

"Lighten up! Papa's just mad no one took the blame for wrecking the sundial."

"Then why is he mad at me? I didn't do it," said Rory.

"I don't know. Who cares? Tomorrow is adventure day!"

"You and your stupid 3-D Amazer. Don't you care about anything else?"

"Like what?"

Rory lowered his voice. "It feels like everyone is keeping secrets. Gran usually tells us everything—don't you think it's weird?"

"Gran is *always* weird," said Morgan.

"This is different. Something's bothering her, and she and Papa are always arguing. It can't just be about me talking to Mr. Glee."

Morgan paused. "Weren't you scared of that bird?"

"A little," said Rory, shrugging.

Morgan picked up a ring to toss over the hazelnut. "I'm going to talk to a *goat* today!"

"Don't you ever want to do something important?" said Rory.

Morgan looked confused.

"I mean, what if we looked for Grampa?"

"Grampa's dead, Rory. Admit it for once!"

"You don't know that."

"Well I know he didn't come back home, so…figure it out."

"Maybe he couldn't. Maybe he needs help!"

"And maybe Wally's a genius."

Rory sighed and lay back. Morgan threw the ring and it circled the hazelnut perfectly, landing lightly in the sand.

"Wing-nut!" Bimble ran outside, Mama and Papa following.

"We'll play later, Bimble." Morgan tugged his sister's ear as he jumped into the wheelbarrow. Papa lifted the handles and rolled him past the mountain of Juneberries.

"When we come back, we'll all help squash these berries into juice," said Mama, following Papa. Rory watched them ramble down the hill.

Gran appeared at the door. "Come on, Bimble, let's go find more berries." She looked over at Rory with pity. "Last day being grounded, right?" She moved toward the far end of the yard where the buckets were stacked.

"Gussie!"

Gran turned her head. Miss Creemore was puffing up the hill as if she'd been running a long way. When she finally reached Gran, she said something quietly in her ear. Gran immediately grabbed Bimble's paw and followed Miss Creemore down the hill again.

"What's going on?" Rory called after her.

"Oh, nothing—she just found a *huge* patch of berries!"

Rory rolled his eyes. Was there *ever* a time when everyone was normal? He looked up at the sky, wishing he could go back to the days when Grampa was around; those seemed like happier times. But all he could really remember of Grampa was the tickle of his whiskers when he used to carry Rory outside to look for the moon as a baby. Everything else he knew about his grandfather was from the stories Gran told, after Grampa was gone. She did her best to tell the twins every detail she could about their grandfather, but she never did say what actually happened to him. On that topic, she had few words.

When Rory grew older and more inquisitive about his grandfather's disappearance, Gran would take him outside to look for the moon, like Grampa had done. "See how the clouds move over the moon?" she would say. "Looks like it vanishes completely, doesn't it? But it's always there, Rory. It's always there." And that's all she could bring herself to say.

Rory tramped inside the house. He was tired of being treated like a baby—no one ever explained anything properly to him. As he headed for the pantry to find a snack, his eye caught the map on the wall. All those places to explore on this beautiful day…he wished he could have at least gone berry-picking.

And then it hit him. Gran hadn't taken a bucket. She wasn't going berry-picking at *all*.

ᘏ

Rory left the scorching pathway and pushed through the reeds into the cool shade of the bog. He had to find Gran and find out what was going on. But where to look? Miss Creemore was tired from running, so she must have taken Gran somewhere farther than the school. He thought back to the map. Miss Bucket! She was the only other mouse who was friends with his family. He remembered seeing her name written along the cliff edge at a bend in the river, north of the bog.

Rory took in a breath and puffed out his cheeks. He would have to cut through the bog, so no one could see him—he was supposed to be grounded, after all. He exhaled and picked up a twig. He mustn't get lost this time.

All was quiet, with no life around. Even the reeds were paralyzed in the breathless heat. Rory crept carefully onward, dragging the twig through the gravel behind him to mark his way. He looked for familiar landmarks from the last time he was there, but the reeds had grown over any semblance of a path. Was that the rock he'd sat by when he first met Mr. Glee?

A sudden voice rang out and he stopped to listen. No—*two* voices. They sounded lazy—it could only be Mack and Jack. Rory was curious to see what their boat was like. Papa said it was unnatural for mice to live on the water, but they seemed to survive just fine.

Rory scrambled under a thicket and peered through the thorny bushes. The afternoon sun fell on the pool where he had helped Glee save his raft. Tiny minnows now jumped in its place, chasing their dinner flies. The boat was easy to find once Rory picked up the unmistakeable odor of unwashed fur. There it was, to the left— Mack and Jack's sailing ship, a human toy escaped from Biggle's pond on a rush of storm water down the old streambed, years ago.

Its limp sails were stained and the white deck paint chipped, but it was still a marvelous sight. Water ripples reflected on its red shiny hull. A rope rail looped through metal poles around the deck, and white rubber fenders shaped like teardrops hung from the poles, nearly touching the water. On the side of the bow, Rory could just make out the name in faded yellow letters: *Where the Wind Blows*. A tingle went up his spine as he imagined being as free as that.

The stern of the boat was loosely tied with a frayed rope around a rock at the edge of the pool. Mack and Jack lay near the mouth of the hold, belly up, in the shade of the sail.

"This is the life, eh?" said Jack.

"Yep," said Mack, yawning.

"I'm going down for a snack. I'm starving."

Jack fumbled frontward down a narrow ladder into the hold, his tail thumping along the rungs behind him.

Rory could hardly believe how simply they lived. There was nothing on deck but two lumpy sacks they used as beds.

"Last of the Juneberries," said Jack, reappearing. He tossed a berry into Mack's lap. A puff of air luffed the mainsail and rippled through the fabric, revealing a tear in one corner. "I suppose we should try to fix that sometime."

The boom swayed slowly over the deck, nearly grazing Mack's mountainous belly. "No rush," he said through a mouthful of berries.

Rory thought the orphan brothers got along remarkably well. Maybe life was easier without parents around. But after minutes of deafening silence, he was glad of the quest that awaited him: he had to find Gran. He followed the pond's shoreline, which took him to the north side of the bog.

Where the bog ended, the river grew close, though it was no threat to Rory. It meandered lazily along the bank, which rose steeply out of the water. A row of weeping willows dangled over the edge, their parched leaves reaching for a drink. Rory ran up the bank and under the trees. He'd never been under a willow tree before. He liked the security of the soft branches swaying all around him, and the sound of his own feet rustling through the fallen leaves.

"Here comes the bird-lover!" A high-pitched squeal rang out, ruining the peace. "Watch out—if he finds out where you live, he'll send his bird-friend after you!"

Tamrin was playing hide-and-seek with some younger mice in the underground passages that wove in and out of the tree roots. The younger mice gasped in horror and hid below ground but Tamrin stood tall, watching Rory curiously as he hurried by.

At the end of the willows, the bank stretched into open air again and curved high around a bend in the river. This was where the map showed Miss Bucket's home, somewhere along the cliff. Rory scrambled back and forth along the edge, but he couldn't see a mouse hole anywhere. He stretched over the edge, looking down at the cove below.

"What are you looking for?" Tamrin yelled from the willows, spooking Rory. He lost his footing and slipped off the edge of the cliff, tumbling all the way down to the beach.

The river lapped quietly at the pebbles. Rory got up to wash himself off when an echoing squeak came from above. He looked up, expecting to see Tamrin again, but instead he noticed a large plateau halfway up the cliff face, atop a steep rock that jutted out from the bank. The voice had come from up there.

The mud was too loose to scramble up again, so Rory had to try his luck at rock-climbing. He clung to the narrow cracks in the sheer face. He didn't dare look down as he pulled himself higher and higher. When he finally reached the top, he slapped his paw to his forehead—there in front of him was a tiny stairwell that switch-backed neatly down the cliff to the plateau! He might have found it if Tamrin hadn't startled him.

The stairs ended at the entrance to a small round tunnel. Rory ran toward the hole, but then stopped as Papa's warnings to be careful rushed into his head. He looked up. There were dozens of similar holes along the top of the cliff—none of which were marked on the map. What lived inside *those*? He was about to lose heart when another squeak came from deep inside the tunnel. This one *had* to be a mouse hole.

Rory crept inside, his eyes wide open in the dark. A thudding sound came from somewhere close by and he stood still to listen. As he held his breath he realized it was his own heart, beating fast. He inched farther along, moving more slowly as the tunnel grew darker.

An arc of yellow light finally appeared up ahead. It seemed like it was coming from a round door, slightly open. As he leaned toward it, his nose hit the doorknob—it was closer than he thought. He heard the squeak again and instantly drew back. Whose voice was *that*? Instead of knocking, he crouched down in the shadows and listened.

"I should know not to go out by myself." The mystery voice sounded old and shredded.

"You can't blame yourself." Rory recognized Miss Creemore's voice. He perked up his ears.

"She's right." This time it was Gran's voice. "You couldn't know what would happen."

Rory's eyes widened. He cupped his ear against the door.

"Maybe now that you're feeling better, you can tell us how you returned in such a state," continued Gran.

"I hardly know where I am," said the strange voice.

"You're at my place." Miss Bucket chimed in.

"So what did happen, dear?" coaxed Miss Creemore. Rory leaned in closer.

"My mind is old and hazy now." There was a long silence before the voice spoke again. "Where's young Willis?"

"That's what we're trying to find out. Remember? He's gone," said Gran, sounding impatient.

"Gone? Nonsense. My little brother can't go out by himself."

"Willis is an old mouse now," said Miss Creemore. "Near as old as you, Hazel."

Great-Aunty *Hazel*? Grampa's sister? Rory looked through the crack of the doorway near the hinge. He could only see a sliver of the old mouse's face. She was lying in a bed while someone's paw adjusted a blanket below her chin. A tuft of white fur glowed hopefully between her ears, but she had hardly any whiskers left and her nose was shriveled and dull.

Rory pulled back from the door. Gran had always told them Aunty Hazel died long ago. Why would she lie about that?

DECISIONS

R ory stared through the crack in the door. Aunty Hazel suddenly began to cough, throwing back the blankets as she sat up to reach for a cup nearby. He could see that her tail was torn off, the stump just beginning to heal.

Aunty Hazel took a sip of water. "How long have I been away from Weedle River, then?" she croaked.

Gran tucked her back in bed. "Many seasons now. Rory and Morgan were just babies."

"Who?"

"My grandsons," said Gran sadly.

Rory moved out of the shadows and peered into the room where the door was ajar. Bimble was sitting on the floor, building a teetering structure out of twigs. Gran sat on a stool beside the bed with her shoulders hunched. Miss Bucket stood behind her and patted her back consolingly. Miss Creemore spoke gently from the opposite side of the bed. "Hazel, can you remember your last day in Weedle River?"

"Yesterday!" Aunty Hazel's voice grew stronger. Gran put her head in her paws, frustrated.

"No, no." Miss Creemore tried again. "I meant the day of your last adventure. Do you remember that?"

"I remember Willis couldn't come with me....something about a grandson."

Rory stiffened.

"That's right," said Gran excitedly as she took Aunty Hazel's paw. "Willis and I took Rory out, just the three of us."

"Who's Rory?" said Hazel, lifting her head off the pillow.

Miss Creemore shook her head at Gran. "Never mind, dear," she said to Aunty Hazel. "So, you were saying you went out alone.... Where did you go?"

Aunty Hazel stared up at the ceiling. "The air was so crisp! I couldn't stay home. So I jumped into the pannier of a motorbike and went into town."

"You went to Eekum-Seekum?" said Miss Creemore.

"Oh, no! I'd been there a hundred times—what a bore! No, that day I went farther."

"Where?" demanded Gran. Miss Creemore gave her a warning look.

"I went to Grule in a fancy basket!"

Gran stood up. "I knew it!"

"So excitable, Gussie!" said Aunty Hazel, with a glint in her eye. "But I'd been to Grule before."

"You had?" Gran froze.

"Oh yes! Many times, on my very own bicycle!" Aunty Hazel closed her eyes and squealed like a giddy lunatic. Gran sat back down, defeated.

"You mustn't push her, Gussie," whispered Miss Creemore. "This is the first time she's spoken and her mind is weak. She doesn't know half of what she's saying."

"I know, I *know*. But it's been over a week now and there are so many questions that must be answered! Where did they take her? Did Willis go too? How did she escape? Did he escape too?" Gran sighed heavily.

Rory leaned against the tunnel wall, half in and half out of the light coming from the door. Grampa could really be alive! How could Gran have kept this secret from him?

"Rowy?" Bimble pushed the door open wider.

"*Shh*. I'm not here," whispered Rory, shifting out of the light.

"But I see you."

"Go back inside before they notice." He waved her away.

"You play hide and seek?"

"*Yes*. Now *go*."

Bimble darted back inside and the door swung closed, leaving Rory in complete darkness. His head burst with angry thoughts. Why hadn't Gran told him what was going on? Nobody ever told him the truth! He ran back up the tunnel.

When he reached the entrance, he immediately ducked back inside.

Hundreds of white-throated birds flew overhead, swooping down to catch mosquitoes along the cliff. The din of chirping chicks was deafening. Those other holes at the top of the cliff were swallows' nests!

Rory's heart skipped as he glanced back down the tunnel. A glimmering light grew closer.... Gran was coming after him. He leapt onto the stairwell up the cliff. He'd rather face the birds than Gran.

"Rory, wait!" she called. "Let me explain!"

Rory kept climbing, digging his claws into the hardened mud. A swallow's wing brushed his face as the birds dived all around him, their babies screeching madly to be fed. Rory stopped, dizzy.

Gran clambered after him with a lantern in her paw. She stopped a few stairs below her grandson.

Rory turned to look at her, hot tears rolling down his face. "How could you lie to me?" he said.

"I couldn't tell you Hazel was alive. Your father wouldn't let me." Gran blew the lantern out. "It was for the best—she's in no state to be part of the family again."

"She looks fine to me."

"She's lost her mind, Rory. She says horrifying things you shouldn't hear."

"I'm old enough now—I want the truth! What happened to her?" Rory wasn't going to give up this time.

Gran paused and looked away before turning to face him again. "The night before your last day of school, Miss Creemore found

Hazel in the pasture. She was face down in the grass and unconscious, her tail torn to shreds. Miss Creemore came to tell your
parents and me, after you were all in bed. Papa swore us to secrecy,
afraid other Weedle Mice would say it proved our adventures would
bring danger to the community. Miss Bucket's was the most seclud-
ed place to hide her, so Papa took Hazel there to rest. Today Miss
Creemore came to find me because your aunty finally spoke. I think
she knows where your grandfather is."

"But Papa said he was killed!"

"I'm old enough now—I want the truth!"

"Yes—that's what your father has always assumed. But—" Gran put the lantern down and took a step upward, putting her paw on Rory's arm. "Hazel and Grampa were actually—"

Rory held his breath.

"Abducted."

Rory looked at Gran in disbelief. "Kidnapped! How do you know?"

"Because I saw it."

"You *saw* what happened to Grampa and you never told me?"

"I—I couldn't tell you."

"Why?"

"You were just a baby, Rory."

"I'm not a *baby* anymore." Rory shook his grandmother's paw off his arm.

Gran sighed quietly. "Grampa was supposed to take Hazel out that day, but he couldn't. We had to…well, we just couldn't. We should've known she'd go anyway. We saw her in town, as we were running under the bushes toward the museum in Seekum. There she was, up ahead, wandering unknowingly into a trap—a *live* trap, thank goodness, but nonetheless. As soon as the trap door fell, a Human appeared, lifted it up, and put another trap down in its place. Your grandfather ran ahead to save her. I remember the museum clock chiming loudly overhead; I had to yell over the noise to beg him not to go, but he was determined to follow her. He ran into the second trap."

"So *that's* what you were mumbling about when you hit your

head at the market," said Rory.

"I followed the Human, but I could only go so far. He put the cages into a van and drove away—I wish I knew where. If I'd let myself be trapped too, I might have been able to help them escape somehow. But—" She stopped.

"But what? Gran, tell me." Rory looked at her intently.

She almost whispered her reply. "I had you on my back. And you were more important to me than anything else in the world."

Rory's eyes grew wide. "I was *there* when Grampa disappeared?"

"Yes. We took you out alone that day because you were upset. The only thing that calmed you was to go on an adventure with just the two of us, so we took you out instead of Hazel."

"*I'm* the reason she and Grampa were lost?" Rory's voice trembled.

"No! I made the choice not to go after them. Your parents trusted me with you and I couldn't fail them. You were so young—how could I risk your life?"

Rory sat back on his haunches. After all this time wondering what really happened, *he* was the reason Grampa was missing. The swallows grew blurry through his tears. They were settling into their nests now, their chicks gone quiet.

Gran lifted his chin with her paw. "It's not your fault, Rory."

"But *why* were they kidnapped?" His curiosity swelled again.

"I don't know. It's strange, but I swear that Human was waiting for us."

"Why would a Human want *us*?"

"That's what I'm hoping Hazel will explain." Gran nudged Rory to get up.

"Why don't we look for Grampa? We can't wait for Aunty Hazel to get better. He might be in danger *now!*"

Gran thought for a moment but didn't reply.

"Let's go!" Rory persisted.

"No, no…. Your father is probably right—we should wait until Hazel speaks some sense. Come on, let's get Bimble and go home before your parents begin to wonder where we are."

Mama and Morgan were in an old margarine tub, busily squashing Juneberries under their feet when Gran, Rory, and Bimble arrived home.

"You missed the coolest thing!" Morgan called out as he jumped up and down.

"Oh yes?" said Gran. She and Bimble climbed into the tub to join them. Rory sat down on one of the lounge chairs.

"Tell!" said Bimble, tugging at Morgan's elbow.

"I was running ahead of Papa and Mama on the way home from the field when a bird swooped down and landed in front of me. I thought it was going to eat me!"

"Did it?" asked Gran, sarcastically.

"No-o-o!" laughed Morgan, his voice wobbling with each jump. "It was Mr. Glee! I asked him, 'What do you want?' He didn't say anything, but he dropped a scarf in front of me and bowed. I said, 'That's Rory's scarf, not mine!' But all he did was push your scarf at me with his beak. I told him I wasn't you, because *I* can find seeds without stealing them. He must have finally understood, 'cause then he said, 'Say hello to your brother for me,' and flew off. Stupid bird—you and I don't look anything alike!"

"What a kind animal," said Gran. "You should pay him more courtesy."

Morgan kept jumping happily up and down. "I can make friends with birds too!"

"Doesn't sound like it," said Rory.

"Come on, Rory, help us squash the berries," said Mama.

"I—can't," he said, trying to hide his scraped paws.

"What happened to you?" Morgan said suspiciously.

"Oh. I, uh…fell into some thorns."

"Where were you, anyway? You're supposed to be grounded!"

"It's all right, Morgan. I took him for a walk with Bimble and me," said Gran quickly.

"I saw Mack and Jack's boat," said Rory.

"You did?" Morgan stopped jumping.

"Yeah. It's great. They do whatever they want all day long."

"So it's pretty cool, huh," said Morgan slowly.

"Yup. I wish I could sail a boat on Biggle's pond," said Rory.

"You'll do no such thing! Your grandfather tried to do that once and nearly drowned." Mama smiled despite her reprimand.

Gran laughed. "Oh, he was fine. I threw a twig out to him and he eventually floated ashore. What a soppy mess he was. He shivered for a week!"

Morgan jumped up and down again. "I'm going to sail a boat before you do, Rory!"

"No sir, you will not!" said Mama. "I'd rather take you all to Grule than let you near Biggle's boats!"

"*No one* is going to the World Beyond." Papa appeared in the doorway. Everyone stopped jumping.

"Ah, thought you'd finally join us?" said Gran, landing on a large juicy berry. It spurted in Papa's face and Bimble squealed with laughter.

"Thought you'd finally come home?" said Papa, licking the berry off his cheek with a half-smile. He climbed into the tub.

Rory watched his family pulverize the berries until they were completely separated into juice and pulp.

❦

After dinner, Mama and Papa busied themselves in the pantry while Morgan and Bimble played Ring-nut outside in the last light of the evening. Gran rested in the velvet chair with her eyes closed and her feet up by the fire, savoring the warmth on her arthritic feet.

Rory lay on his bed and watched the flames curl and jump. He wondered where Papa would take them on their adventure the next day—probably never far enough to find Grampa. He tiptoed into the kitchen to look at the map.

Papa's tail trailed out the doorway of the pantry, where he and Mama quietly packaged the berry paste by candlelight, their long shadows wavering on the wall. Rory quickly traced the river on the map with his paw…. Under the bridge, past Biggle's farm, along the highway, through Eekum-Seekum, and then—nothing. According to his parents' map, this was their entire world. But it wasn't big enough for Rory. He wondered how far the river went and where it really ended.

As he climbed back on his bed, his claw caught on a corner of the book of fables that stuck out from underneath. He picked it up and the pages immediately fell open to "The Proud Mouse and the Trap." A familiar shiver went up his spine as he read it again:

> There was a proud old mouse from the country
> who often went to town to brag about himself.
> One day, he stood on the steps outside the Museum
> of Zoology…

Rory sat up. Gran said Grampa was caught at the museum in Seekum. He continued:

> There was such a commotion of squeaks that even
> the Humans began to notice…

Rory leaned over the book. Could this be the Human Gran spoke of? He leapt off the bed and scurried to the fireplace with the book.

"Gran," he whispered. She was wheezing lightly with her head slumped to one side. He shook her arm.

"What is it?" She stirred, annoyed.

"Remember the book of fables I got at the market? Read this one, here. Quick!"

"What's the rush? I was sleeping!"

"It's got to do with what we were talking about earlier," he said quietly.

Gran snatched the book. Her ears curled forward as she followed the words with her claw on the page.

"You said a Human caught Aunty Hazel and Grampa in live traps outside the museum, right?" whispered Rory.

Gran flipped the page. There was a paragraph about the author on the inside cover of the book. "How would a mouse from Grule know this story? Unless Grule *is* where they were taken...." She looked at Rory and clapped the book shut. "We've got to keep this secret from your father. Do not tell him what you heard or saw today. Understand? I need to find out more about this and I can't do it with him watching over me. He never listens to a word I say—he *still* thinks Grampa is dead! When you go on your family adventure tomorrow, I'll take this book to Hazel. Maybe it will jog her memory. And if it doesn't, I'm going to go find your grandfather anyway."

"I want to help you!"

"No. You're too young."

The fur on Rory's neck stood up. "I am *not* too young."

Gran considered her grandson. His tail flicked as he waited for her to respond. Its stripes were darkening nicely, and it had grown quite long over the winter.

"I'm helping you and that's final." Rory put his paw on hers and squeezed it.

"Helping her do what?"

Rory whipped his head around. Morgan was standing in the doorway.

"How long have you been listening?" said Rory.

Morgan shrugged. "Long enough."

"Rory wants to help me collect berries from now on," said Gran. "I'm getting old." She leaned down to rub her foot.

"She needs us to help out more," said Rory, going along with Gran.

"Hmm," said Morgan. He turned his head outside again. "Come on inside, Bimble. It's dark." Bimble dashed by and into the kitchen. Morgan eyed Rory suspiciously before following his sister.

"I'm not sure he believed us," whispered Rory.

"I hope he did. I don't want Morgan involved. He'd be sure to tell your father, and then we'd be finished. Papa would never let us go anywhere off the map."

Rory could hear Papa and Mama in the kitchen now, scrubbing

their berry-stained paws in the sink. Mama poked her head through to the living room.

"You two want to join us for some juice? Then it's time for bed. We need to rest up for our adventure tomorrow."

Rory helped Gran get up from the chair. As she shuffled off to the kitchen, he stuffed the book under the bed. Gran was right—Morgan mustn't find out. He'd tell Papa for sure, and that would ruin everything.

Rory joined everyone in the kitchen and sat down next to Gran.

"So we're not going to the market?" said Morgan, disappointed.

"No," said Papa. "You don't need another maze game. Your mother and I decided we'd go farther tomorrow. Not too far, just a bit." He looked at Gran warily. "I suppose you still refuse to come?"

"Like I said, your idea of *adventure* is as dull as dishwater," Gran muttered.

"We've decided to go to the museum in Seekum," said Mama cheerily.

"Moozeem?" said Bimble.

Rory kicked Gran under the bench, and she winked back at him. "Maybe I'll come after all."

Morgan watched Gran and Rory intently as he drank the rest of his juice.

✦TEN✦

DIVIDING INTERESTS

When the Stowaways rose at dawn, it was already hot. After a quick breakfast, they packed their pouches and headed toward the shadier side of the farm. They scrambled up the old streambed, under the fence, and through the pasture until it ended at Biggle's Pond.

Morgan slowed to look at the human toy sailboats. There were four of them moored to a wooden wharf that stretched out from the bank. The water level was low from the past week of sun, and the boats were well beneath dock height. He ran down the wharf and bent over the edge to look at them. Their hulls were yellow, green, blue, and white. Each boat had a mainsail and a smaller jib. He studied the ropes to see how they worked. They were coiled around a winch on the deck that kept the sails from moving. His eyes fell on the green boat—it was definitely the finest, a proper pond boat with a wooden wheel at the stern. He leaned down to spin it. It worked! The boat moved well to the left.

"Can we try sailing?" Morgan called.

"No," said Papa. "And get back here."

"The water's shallow. I won't drown," said Morgan, running back up the wharf.

"*No.*" Papa pushed him ahead as he led the family around a flock of ducks, still asleep on the grass with their bills tucked under their wings.

To get to the road, they had to pass through the petting zoo, which wasn't open to the public yet. The furry white cow, the brown speckled pig, the fat donkey, and the miniature horses all faced the gate, quietly awaiting the impending crowd of children. Unnoticed, the Stowaways slipped through their pens and then headed across the parking lot and down the driveway.

"Another bulldozer!" said Morgan excitedly when they reached the road. The Stowaways readied themselves to board it.

"I don't trust Humans, always pushing the earth around with their big machines, fixing what isn't broken." Papa looked west toward the bridge over the river, where the Humans were rebuilding the south wall again.

"I thought you'd be glad of the safe ride," said Gran, rolling her eyes.

The bulldozer drew close. Morgan was the first to jump on. "Come on, Ror, let's ride on the crawler again!"

"I'm staying down here this time," said Rory, sitting next to Gran on the bar between the wheels.

Morgan looked at Rory for a second. His brother seemed more

anxious than usual today. "Suit yourself," he said, swinging overhead.

The bulldozer eventually arrived in Eekum, where it kept to the side of the main street that led down to the river. When it slowed to turn right toward the dockyards, the Stowaways jumped off. They stood near the intersection at the foot of the drawbridge leading to Seekum.

"That's where we're going," said Gran, pointing across the river to the museum.

Morgan stared up at the building's clock tower. A weathervane at the top creaked eerily as it turned slightly northwest, sending shivers down his spine. He wished they could go somewhere fun. He didn't want to *muse* at things; he wanted to play with them.

"As a little detour," said Papa, pointing to a small brick building across the street, "we'll go through Sparkle's Toyshop before crossing the bridge. But we have to be quick. The shop opens soon and we want to avoid the trample of children's fee—"

"A toyshop?" Morgan took off like a shot.

"Look out!" Mama shouted. A car reversed into a parking spot in front of the shop, the rolling tire just missing Morgan's tail as he sped underneath and ran up the curb.

"Stay there!" yelled Papa. The rest of the Stowaways ran through the drain grate under the street and climbed up the curb from the gutter on the other side.

"Don't ever do that again!" said Papa.

"You were taking so *long*," said Morgan.

"We stick together on adventures, and that's final," said Papa.

"All right, all right—he gets the point," said Gran. She looked up at the brass mail slot in the toyshop door. "Is that the only way in?"

"We can squeeze underneath," said Mama. The green wooden door had shrunk with age and didn't fit tightly in the frame. Mama unwound Bimble's bindings so Papa could fit through the crack at the threshold. Morgan raced ahead and ran under the door, followed by Gran and Rory.

"Who told them they could go ahead?" said Papa. The car door opened and a human foot landed near his head.

"Good thing they did," said Mama. "Let's get out of here." They dashed across the sidewalk. Mama led Bimble under the door and Papa followed, pushing hard to get through. A heavy flap on the other side made the way tight.

"They put a weather strip around the door," said Mama, as she lifted Bimble onto Papa's back again. "We won't be able to get out this way again."

"Hmm," said Papa, trying to push the stiff rubber back the other way, unsuccessfully. "We'll have to use the cat flap in the back door of the storeroom. Let's hope that beast isn't roaming the alley today."

The sun shone through butter-colored blinds pulled down over the front window, giving the toyshop a warm, cosy glow. High shelves held books, games, puzzles, and kits, lining the walls from front to back and floor to ceiling. Morgan spun around to take it all in, but he couldn't see much from the floor. He felt small.

"Look at all the eyes everywhere," said Rory, recoiling from an entire shelf of slouching rag dolls staring blindly down at them.

"Nothing's alive in here, Ror. Take it easy," teased Morgan. He dashed over to a tall plush animal near the window. It was beige and covered in a mosaic of brown patches, with an impossibly long neck that reached almost to the ceiling, and legs even taller than reeds. Morgan climbed up to one of its bulbous cheeks, where he rested in the hollow under a giant blue eye. He had a much better view from here.

Mama and Papa crossed the floor to a bookcase and climbed to the top, where they pulled themselves onto a ledge that carried a toy train track all the way round the room. Bimble waved across to Morgan.

Rory and Gran climbed up to the window display beneath Morgan. Dozens of marionettes hung over their heads, their limbs held by strings suspended from the ceiling. Nearest to Morgan were the strings controlling a boy puppet with a long nose and an old man puppet in breeches.

"Watch this, Ror!" Morgan reached out and yanked on a string.

Down below, the boy spun around so fast that his legs splayed out like helicopter blades and kicked the old man behind the knee. The old man's boot flew off and hit Gran in the belly. Morgan stifled a giggle.

"Hey!" said Gran, smiling. She threw the boot up to Morgan. "Show some respect for your elders!"

Morgan played the strings like a harp. The puppets bobbed up and down in a silly dance, twirling and bowing to Rory and Gran, who doubled over with laughter.

"Do it again!" cried Rory.

But Morgan had seen something better. He scrambled down the giraffe and ran to a table in the middle of the room. He climbed up a leg and pulled himself up. On the tabletop sat a yellow wooden dollhouse, three stories high with blue shuttered windows, and a steep shingled roof with dormers. He looked up in awe.

"This is *way* bigger than our house!"

"Looks like you'll have to share it," said Mama, laughing from the ledge above. Morgan looked around. A family of stiff-looking mice stood nearby. He poked one lightly and it teetered. It was just a toy made of fuzzy gray plastic.

"They look a little like us," said Rory, when he and Gran joined Morgan on the table.

Gran examined another toy mouse in a floral dress with green plastic spectacles glued to its face. "This must be where town mice get their clothes." She frowned as she tugged at a lace cuff around its wrist. "Oh!" The toy's arm moved down.

"They have joints," said Morgan, more interested now. He moved toward a small toy mouse in overalls, perched on a red contraption with two gray wheels.

"It's a bicycle," said Gran. Morgan tried to spin the front wheel, but it wouldn't budge. He moved the toy's foot off the pedal and pushed down on it. The wheel nudged forward. He pushed the toy mouse off the seat and climbed on.

"Morgan!" Papa called down. "Get off that thing—you don't know how to ride it!" He and Mama meandered along the train track on the ledge overhead. "I don't understand it," said Papa, stopping at a shiny red train in their way. "We raised those boys to be sensible, but every chance they get, they do the most foolish things."

"Oh, well. Let's have a bit of fun too, shall we?" Mama hung on to a bar on the side of the train and pushed off with her foot. The train jerked forward.

"Ride!" said Bimble. Papa reluctantly boarded the caboose while Mama pushed off again. The train went a little faster and Bimble squealed.

Morgan grabbed the handlebars and leaned forward, stepping down hard on the pedals. The bicycle shot forward and he fell to one side.

"Be careful!" Papa stared down while Mama paddled the track with her foot.

"Oh, let him try," she said. The train picked up speed as it turned round a corner.

"Wheeeee!" cried Bimble, her ears flapping in the breeze.

"Try it again, Morg!" said Rory.

Morgan picked up the bike and climbed on again. Gran held the back of the seat and gave him a push. He wobbled around the yard, bumping the toy mice off the table one by one.

"Be nice, now!" laughed Gran.

Morgan gained speed and whipped around the side of the doll-house, getting the hang of it. "I'm taking this home!"

"Morgan, look out!" Papa shouted down from the ledge as the storeroom door flew open.

"Eeee!" A human cry tore across the room. "Mice!"

"Hide!" yelled Papa. Morgan threw the bike down and dashed for cover, but there was nowhere to hide. The back of the dollhouse was wide open, with no walls to close it in. He flew up a set of narrow stairs past two floors to the attic, where he was fully covered under the roof. He crouched inside a dormer and peered out the window. A young girl with a mischievous look on her face stood in the doorway to the storeroom.

The train slowed to a halt overhead and the girl looked up. She hopped over to a switch on the wall, reached up, and flicked it. The train began to move again, much faster this time.

Mama pulled in her foot and nervously looked back at Papa as the train carried them helplessly around the room. The girl laughed giddily.

"*Psst*! Morgan!"

Morgan crossed the attic to the opposite dormer. Rory and Gran were crouched below, hidden under an artificial bush. Morgan snapped the window grill, and climbed out the dormer onto the roof. He carefully crawled down the front of the doll house and joined Rory and Gran.

"What do we do?" he whispered.

"Run!" Gran grabbed her grandsons and pushed them onto the table leg, which they slid down like a fire pole. "Behind the counter!" She pointed to the cash desk, but the girl was already on them.

"Hah!" she screamed.

"Right!" cried Gran.

"Left!" yelled Morgan.

"Under here!" shouted Rory.

Running in circles, they desperately searched for a place to hide as the girl fumbled after them.

"Jump the train!" yelled Papa.

Morgan looked up as he ran. As the train passed over the storeroom door, his parents leapt off, rolling sideways toward the edge of the shelf. They clutched the ledge with their claws, saving themselves from a terrifying drop to the floor. Bimble pitched forward through Papa's ears, heading for a fall.

"Bimble!" Morgan stopped running.

"Look out!" Rory yelled as the girl's hand swooped down over Morgan's head, just missing him. Morgan ran behind the cash counter after Gran and Rory, then peered out around the corner. Papa had just caught Bimble by the paw.

Relieved, Morgan slouched down and sighed. "Phew!" He

watched Mama strap Bimble in place then lead Papa stealthily down the bookcase.

"Aren't *you* special." A blast of hot breath wilted the fur on Morgan's back. The Human girl was bent over him, poised for a swipe. Gran snatched Morgan's arm and pulled him far behind the counter, out of sight. Morgan began to shake all over—he'd never been in real danger before. He looked over at Rory. Why didn't his brother look scared?

"Stay still," said Gran. Morgan froze. Over the noise of the train rushing around the room, he could hear the sound of a stool dragging clumsily across the floor. What was that girl *doing*?

Gran called Rory to her and they whispered together, nodding.

"Come on, Morgan!" Gran suddenly shouted. Morgan scrambled to his feet as Gran and Rory shot out from the counter and ran toward the storeroom. Mama and Papa reached the floor and joined them as they headed for the back door. Morgan fell behind, his heart thumping.

"You're mine!" The girl jumped down from the stool with a fishnet in her hand. She swiped at Morgan wildly, catching his ear on the rim of the net. He stumbled sideways.

"Run, Morgan!" yelled Mama. Morgan caught a glimpse of his mother as she ducked behind a box. The net swooped down at him again. He lunged forward and dashed under a pile of green plastic water pistols just inside the storeroom. He caught his breath and

"You're mine!"

looked around for his family.

The storeroom was filled with boxes and junk. All he could see was a dark musty staircase leading upstairs. He sniffed at the air. What was that smell? Did the girl torture frogs up there or something? He wouldn't be surprised—

The little girl stomped into the room. "Here mousey, mousey!"

Morgan dodged farther under the pile of water pistols, shifting them noisily.

"Aha!" The girl waded in after him, toppling over the pile with a loud racket. Heavy footsteps thumped across the floor above.

"What are you doing down there?" A voice boomed down the stairway.

"Nothing…," said the girl, stopping in her tracks.

Morgan finally saw the back door. Papa and Mama were leaning through a cat flap, waving at him to hurry through. He darted out of the pile.

"Hey!" The girl lunged at him with the net, but he leapt through the cat door just in time.

Morgan had hardly finished slithering into the alley outside when Papa grabbed him by the neck fur. "You gave us a real scare!"

Mama put her arms around her son, hugging him to her. "Thank goodness you're not hurt!"

A barge horn blew loudly in the river nearby. The drawbridge to Seekum rumbled up to let the boat go through, disturbing a flock of perching seagulls, who flew up, crying. Morgan covered his ears. He was ready for a rest after all this excitement.

"The museum will be quieter than this," smiled Mama. "Let's go."

"The only place we're going is home," said Papa. "I knew it was a bad idea to go this far."

"We couldn't know this would happen," said Mama.

"*Precisely*," said Papa.

"We're all fine, right?" She hugged Morgan again.

"Absolutely not. We go back home at once," said Papa. Bimble began to whimper.

"Well, perhaps you're right," said Mama, comforting Bimble. "Let's go home."

Morgan looked around. "Where are Rory and Gran?"

Papa and Mama froze. "The *cat!*"

෨

Rory chased after his grandmother. He had to help her before it was too late. But this was worse than fighting with Wally or befriending a bird—he was going to be in *way* more trouble. Papa might never forgive him.

The road was getting steeper and steeper in front of him and he could feel himself slow down.

"Quick!" Gran yelled back at him.

A horn blew loudly. Rory flinched as he caught up to Gran,

nearly tumbling over the edge of the drawbridge, which was rising up to let a river barge go through. The gap grew wider between them and the other side.

"Can you make it?" said Gran, doubtfully.

Rory looked down. Water gushed angrily around the hull of the idling boat waiting to go through. "It's too far to jump," he said nervously. The other side of the bridge rose higher and higher.

"We'll go over the barge roof," said Gran. When the drawbridge stopped moving, the barge blew its horn again and began to push slowly through the passage. Rory balanced himself on the edge of the bridge as it drew near.

"Now!" They leapt onto the barge. It was moving quicker than Rory thought, and the bridge on the other side would soon fall behind them. They raced diagonally across the roof and leapt off the back corner just before it cleared the bridge, blowing its horn a second time. They pulled themselves over the steep ledge and ran back down the other side, as the bridge slowly lowered and the road flattened out.

Gran stopped under a bush to rest. Rory looked at her anxiously.

"There's plenty of time to get home before dark," said Gran. "Don't worry."

"No—you're right—after what happened in the toyshop, Papa would never have let us go on to the museum. This was our only chance."

Rory knew his parents would worry, but it wouldn't be long before they were together again. They had to find out whatever they could at the museum. Aunty Hazel might take a lifetime to remember where the Humans had taken them, and meanwhile Grampa could be in trouble. They had to act now.

"Let's go," said Gran. The clock tower struck nine as Rory followed her to the museum.

⁓

Mama, Papa, and Morgan peeked out from under a doormat across the alley. The cat stalking by them was nothing like the one at Biggle's farm. Its short, buff hair rippled over its muscled body and its long, dark face loomed under cold blue eyes. As soon as it jumped through the flap and into the toyshop, Mama sat up with a smile.

"That cat hasn't eaten in ages," she said. "I could hear its stomach rumbling. There's no way it just ate Rory and Gran."

Papa crawled out from under the doormat and adjusted Bimble on his back. "Then where did those two get off to?"

"The cat probably chased them down the lane. Let's wait for them to come back."

Morgan looked down the alley, where it ended at the riverside road. A barge horn blew a second time. He could see the drawbridge to Seekum lower down and clang back into place. Something didn't feel right, but he wasn't sure what it was.

ꙮ ELEVEN ꙮ

SEEKUM

R ory stood in the foyer, looking up at a ceiling that was stories overhead. The Museum of Natural Curiosity was the biggest building he'd ever seen. Pillars and archways led down wide hall-ways, which seemed limitless in length. The sun streamed through the windows down the east-wing hall, dividing the floor into stripes of shadow and light. It was beautiful.

"Let's go this way." Gran sniffed the floor as she headed for the east wing. Rory followed, his claws making a *click, click, click* sound on the floor. He could see his reflection in the polished marble as they moved down the empty hall. Though the museum wasn't open yet, Rory thought he heard the faint echo of human footsteps in the distance.

They finally came to a set of heavy wooden doors. Rory stopped to read a sign on the wall: "Winged Vertebrates Of Our Region." He wasn't sure what a *vertebrate* was, but he didn't like the idea of them being winged.

Gran followed her nose under the door and Rory crept in behind her. As soon as he reached the other side, he froze. Hundreds
of birds were in flight above them.

"Gran! Watch out!" He reached for her tail as she moved away
from him.

But Gran was completely unfazed. She climbed up a long vinyl
bench in the middle of the room. "It's all right, Rory. *Look*."

Rory jumped up beside her. He soon realized that clear glass
walls protected and divided them from a diorama that spanned
the entire room under a huge domed ceiling. Beyond the glass, the
walls were painted with scenes of distant lakes, moody skies, and
dense forests, and the floor was covered in dried leaves, brush, and
pine needles. Small birds perched on branches and huddled over
nests in model trees. And pinned in midair above were enormous
birds of prey.

"Can't they see us?" said Rory, ducking under the gaze of a div-
ing hawk.

Gran looked pleased. "They're stuffed," she said.

Rory sniffed the air but there was no scent of any living creature.
Still, it felt unnatural to be viewing all these birds without the threat
of death. One bird alone had a wingspan far greater than their hill,
with claws each as long as his tail.

Gran sniffed along the bench toward the other side of the room.
Rory followed uneasily.

"Have you and Grampa been here before?"

"Oh, yes. He loved to study birds."

"Is this where he got the falcon's talon on our sundial?"

Gran didn't reply. She climbed down the bench to the floor, and slid under the door to the next room.

On the wall next to the door was another sign: "Traveling Exhibits." Rory didn't know what an *exhibit* was, but if it was traveling, he hoped it was behind glass too.

The room behind the door was pitch dark, though a familiar smell began to fill Rory's nostrils. After his eyes adjusted, he could make out a number of dimly lit glass chambers set into the walls.

Gran pointed to a sign on the wall. Rory read it aloud this time: "Regal Rodents: Top Ten Most Curious Species of Mice."

He whispered the last words: "*Live examples.*"

☙

Morgan was mad at Rory for running off and ruining his lunch. Gran had said the museum restaurant was full of exotic food, and he'd been looking forward to some new and scrumptious flavors.

"Can we go to the market?" he said hopefully. "Maybe Gran took Rory back there."

"Buns!" said Bimble.

"Hmm," said Mama distantly. She was looking up and down the empty alley.

Papa sighed. "They probably *did* go back to the market to get another cat tickler, or something equally silly. It isn't far—let's go."

Morgan was ecstatic. "Can we go back through the toyshop so I can take that bicycle home?"

"Don't push your luck!"

✦

"We've got to see inside those chambers," said Gran. Rory followed her up a vinyl cube chair by the door. They craned their necks, but even on the chair, they were too low and too far away.

"You think *Grampa* might be here?" Rory wanted it to be true. But didn't Gran say the Human had driven away with Hazel and Grampa? Why would they bring them back here again?

Gran wrung her tail in her paws. "We don't have much time before the museum opens. You see those angled signs coming out from the wall under each window? We've got to get up on those."

The walls were covered in polished black tiles. "It looks pretty slippery," said Rory. "But maybe we could climb up those pathways." A strip of rough grout ran between the tiles, creating a grid over the walls.

"I can't climb like that. I'm not strong enough anymore," said Gran.

"I can do it," said Rory. He left Gran on the chair and crossed the floor to the first chamber. The tile grout was easy to grip but as narrow as a tightrope. He took off his pouch and laid it down.

With one paw in front of the other, he climbed up the grout. When he reached the plaque, he grabbed the edge and swung his feet up, struggling to cling onto the steep slippery surface.

"Read what it says!" Gran called out.

"'Number ten!" he called back. "*Mus-car-dimus a-vell-an-arius.* Dormouse.'" He read the description. "'Dormice are small rodents, measuring three to seven inches in length. They are deft climbers and have an unusually developed sense of hearing—'"

"Puh," said Gran. "What's so great about that?"

Rory peered into the chamber. A large silvery mouse with a short pink snout lay curled up against the glass in a dell of woodchips. It blinked, revealing an eye nearly as big as its ear, which was small and almost hidden in a roll of fat. It seemed unaware of him. Rory continued to read the text, fascinated that such a strange creature could be called a mouse, even though it looked nothing like him.

"It says here they are eaten in some parts of the world as a delicacy!" Rory was shocked. Humans *ate* mice?

"There's nothing delicate about a dormouse," said Gran impatiently. "Next!"

Rory swung his feet back on the wall and crawled horizontally across the grout. The second chamber was a mess. The woodchips were pushed into mounds and the mouse was nowhere to be seen.

"'Number nine: *Mus spici-leg-us,*'" said Rory carefully. "'Mound-building mouse. Known to—'"

"Spicy legs? Maybe they eat that one too," said Gran. "Next!"

Rory crawled to the next chamber.

"'Number 8: *Mus cookii*,'" said Rory. "'Cook's mouse.'"

"Who knew Humans were so obsessed with eating mice?" said Gran. "Next!"

"'Number Seven: *Mus orangiae*. Orange mouse…. Number Six: *Mus famulus*. Servant mouse…. Number Five: *Mus tenellus*. Delicate mou—'"

"Well, now we've found the real *delicacy*," grumbled Gran. "It's like a menu for a bizarre feast."

As Rory called out the next two mice, Gran barely responded. He wondered if she was giving up hope.

"I don't see them anywhere. What are we going to do?" Mama passed a bit of cinnamon bun up to Bimble, while Morgan stuffed a whole one in his mouth as he eyed the toy stall down the aisle.

"I can't understand why they'd go off on their own," said Papa. He looked down at Morgan. "You don't know anything about this, do you?"

"No," said Morgan, swallowing awkwardly. There *had* been something strange about Rory and Gran last night…but they were always in cahoots over something and never included him, so what would *he* know?

"Gran knows Eekum even better than we do. She'll bring Rory

home, right?" said Mama. Morgan didn't think Mama looked as confident as she sounded.

"I guess we have no choice. We'll have to wait for them at home. But when they get back, that's it—no more adventures, ever!" Papa was really angry.

Morgan supposed he shouldn't ask for another bun.

❧

There were only two chambers left. Rory climbed onto the next plaque and looked through the glass. Inside, a number of mice nested in groups. Some had scraps of fabric hanging off their limbs.

"'Number Two: Mus musculus.'"

"What's that? A weightlifting mouse?" Gran sounded annoyed.

"'Domestic mouse,'" read Rory. He added, "They seem to be wearing fabric."

"A town mouse?" Gran snorted. "That's the second-most unusual mouse, because it's ridiculous enough to wear clothing? I can hardly wait to hear what's in the last chamber." She slumped down with her cheek resting on her paw.

Rory moved quickly to the last chamber. Time was running out before the museum opened. He pulled himself onto the last sign.

"'Number One: Apodemus sylvaticus, virga grandi, senex.'" He looked inside the chamber, but there was no mouse. There weren't even any woodchips.

"Empty!" He called out.

"Empty? Are you sure?" Gran sat up on the chair. "What does the sign say?"

"'Long-tailed field mouse, elderly, of unknown origin. Recently identified as the world's rarest and most unusual species. Only two examples have been found, appropriately...'" He slowed down, reading closer, "'...Here, at the Museum of Natural Curiosity.'"

"WHAT?" Gran scrambled down the chair.

Rory's heart beat quickly as he read on.

"'These mice have unusually large ears, long, furry striped tails, and coats of either gray or brown, with lighter bellies that whiten with age. It is not known how long they live, but it is well beyond the lifespan of other species of mice. Scientists are hoping to find more specimens so they can conduct tests to determine the reason for their longevity. Such information could aid scientists in extending the life expectancy of humans.'"

Sweat crept through Rory's fur. Weedle Mice had been right about one thing—they *were* a special breed. But it wasn't the town mice who were after them; it was the Humans.

Gran crossed the room and climbed slowly up the wall. He helped her onto the plaque. "There's a photo taped inside the glass," she said.

Even in the dark, Rory could see the familiar tuft of white fur on the mouse's forehead. Without a doubt, it was Aunty Hazel.

A handwritten note was taped to the bottom. He read it aloud. "'Mouse has escaped. Reward offered if returned alive.'"

"Good for her!" said Gran, thumping her paw on the glass. "But you know what this means...."

"She and Grampa were kidnapped on purpose, just like you thought?"

Gran nodded, her ears drooping. "And your grandfather is still stuck in a research lab somewhere, undergoing tests."

Rory tried to imagine Grampa imprisoned in a lab. What kind of tests would Humans do on him?

"Maybe he escaped too," he said, hopefully.

"No, there's only a photo of Hazel here. And besides, if your grandfather had escaped, he would have made it back home." Gran whipped her tail in the air.

Rory wondered about that, considering Aunty Hazel's ragged state when she was found. *Would* Grampa have survived if he escaped?

A sudden draft rippled through the fur on his back. The door had been opened behind them. Gran led the way down the wall and across the floor, silently hiding behind the open door. The lights flicked on in the room and the sound of fluorescent bulbs buzzed in his ears. Rory looked out from under the door.

A pair of black shoes kicked a wooden block, which stopped inches from his nose and held the door open. Another Human in gray-heeled shoes sat down with a *pfouff* on the cube chair.

"Have a good day, Ma'am," said a male voice.

"Thanks, dear." The woman sounded older.

The security guard left the room and the museum guide took a thin booklet from her jacket pocket and placed it on her lap, along with a two-way radio.

"We have to find out where the lab is before we leave," said Gran.

"I've read everything in here," said Rory. "There's nothing about where the lab is."

"What did you read about that dormouse again?"

"That Humans eat them?"

"No, before that."

"They have unusually developed hearing."

"Right! I'm going to go talk to that dormouse through the glass, and you're going to distract the guide while I do it," said Gran, pulling off her pouch. Rory was about to protest, but he was too late. She had already dashed across the doorway and under the guide's chair. There was nothing he could do but help her. As soon as he saw Gran appear on the other side of the chair, he sauntered out into the middle of the floor.

"Eek!" shrieked the guide. She grabbed her radio and stood on the chair, her booklet falling to the floor. Rory sat still, feeling quite safe. This woman was no predator, unlike that toyshop girl.

"Mouse!" she screamed into the radio.

Rory meandered around the room, while Gran climbed the wall and began to pound on the glass in front of the dormouse.

Shoes suddenly clacked down the east-wing hall and thudded across the bird-room floor. Rory dashed behind the door again.

"Where's the mouse?" The security guard rushed in.

"I—I don't know. It disappeared!" said the guide, stepping back on the floor. The guard scanned the room.

Rory's stomach clenched. Gran was still in front of the dormouse exhibit, one ear suction-cupped to the glass, her paws waving about in the air.

"*Mouse!*" screamed the guide again, pointing at Gran. "There! It's up on the sign now!" The guard picked the guide's booklet up off the floor and rolled it into a tube.

"Gran, look out!" Rory ran across the doorway and under the chair.

The guard lunged toward Gran with the tube held high like a bat. She turned to climb down the wall, but the guard took a swipe at her and she ducked, taking a flying leap off the plaque. Rory watched in horror as his grandmother hit the floor.

The guard quickly knelt down and scooped Gran up in the tube. Her tail hung down over the edge. The guard touched it curiously. "Hmm…striped," he said. "You'd better go get the cage." He threw a key toward the guide. The guide caught the key and crossed to the wall near the first chamber. With a shaky hand, she put the key in a tiny hole in the wall and turned it. A hidden door swung open.

Rory watched quietly from under the chair, his heart beating rapidly.

A moment later, the guide returned and bent down, putting the key and a metal cage on the floor near the security guard. She stood up and backed away. The guard carefully tilted the tube inside the cage and Gran slid out onto the woodchips. She didn't move.

"Gran?" Rory whispered from under the chair, trying not to squeak too loudly.

The guard touched Gran's neck with two fingers.

"Quite dead?" The guide quaked hopefully.

"Nah. Just a little stunned," pronounced the guard. "Good thing too. It looks like the mouse that escaped."

Rory sighed in relief; there was still a chance for Gran. The guard latched the cage door and lifted it off the floor. Rory watched his shoes move through the hidden doorway. He heard the cage set down on something, then his shoes reappeared.

"Hmm, now where did I put that key…?" said the guard.

"I gave it back to you," said the guide meekly.

Rory's ears perked up. The door was still open! Could he make it there before the guard locked it? He was just about to propel himself at full speed toward the door, when the guard pulled it shut and turned in his direction. Rory ducked back under the chair. Too late!

"I'll get the curator," said the guard. "The mice are going back to the lab tonight, and he'll be anxious to see if this is the missing mouse. Don't worry—I'll be back before you find another one!" He left the room, chuckling.

Voices of museum visitors echoed loudly down the east-wing

hall as Rory's mind raced with images of Gran hitting the floor. How could he have saved her? Grampa would have run inside the cage, just like he had followed Aunty Hazel. Rory pounded the floor with his fist. Why hadn't *he* been brave like that? He took a deep breath. He had to get into that hidden room. If they were taking the mice away tonight, there would be no second chance.

A shrill human voice came from the bird room next door, followed by other voices. Had the guide left the room without him noticing? Rory looked for her shoes, but they were gone.

It was now or never.

He crawled out from the chair and ran to the hidden door. It was so flush with the floor, though, that there were no cracks to squeeze under. He looked up to the keyhole—it was much too small to crawl through.

A series of laughs from the bird room grew louder. Rory glanced back to check for the guide when something shiny caught his eye on the floor.

The security guard's key!

He ran over and picked it up. It was nearly as tall as him, but light enough to carry. He coiled it in his tail and scurried toward the hidden door. As quickly as he could, he scaled the wall.

The keyhole was near the edge of one of the tiles. Rory held onto the grout with his hind feet and unwound the key from his tail. He reached for the keyhole with his front paw, his hind legs quivering with exhaustion.

He put the key in the hole.

Rory pulled and pulled, but it was useless. He wasn't strong enough to turn it. He let his feet go and hung on the key, desperately trying to move it. Then he pushed his feet against the door and tried that way, turning it with all his might. The key just would not budge.

The door, however, did.

As soon as they reached home, Morgan made Bimble a snack. He rolled some crushed seeds and Juneberry paste together to make little fruit balls for her and then sat on the bench across from her, chewing his own food quietly. Mama and Papa stayed outside, raking squashed berries out of the grass while they waited for Rory and Gran to come home. Morgan listened as the metal tines tore through the ground. His parents hadn't said a word on the way home. He'd never seen them like this before—were they angry or sad?

"Rowy and Gran on map?" said Bimble. Morgan looked over at the map on the wall. Eekum didn't seem so far anymore, now that they'd been there twice.

"Yes, they're on the map. And they'll be home soon," said Morgan, smiling. *Probably*, he thought, and the smile left his face. Something was beginning to nag him.

What had Rory and Gran been talking about the night before, when he caught them whispering by the fire?

THE DORMOUSE

Rory could not believe his luck. The hidden door wasn't locked! It had fallen open a crack when he pushed on it with his feet. He squeezed through, slid to the floor, and after a great effort, managed to force the door closed again.

The hidden room was a long, dark hallway that ran behind the mouse chambers. Black canvas hung over the back of each one, covered in air holes through which beams of light pierced the darkness. A wooden table sat against the wall. Rory climbed up a leg and there was Gran, still in the cage. He was relieved to find her so quickly—he would have to get her out of there, fast. The guard said he was coming back soon. Rory lifted the door latch and rustled through the woodchips.

"Gran!" he said, shaking her gently.

When she didn't stir, Rory looked at her more closely. Her arm hung at an odd angle and didn't seem to move with the rest of her body. He shook her again.

"Wake up!"

She moaned, moving slightly as she rubbed a bump on her head. "Ow."

"You're okay!"

"Alive—yes. Where am I?"

In a rush, Rory explained what happened, though Gran could hardly make out his garbled, excited words. "…So now we just have to get out of here before the guard comes back!" Rory finally finished, trying to pull her up. "Come on, let's go!"

"Slow down! My head's throbbing." She brushed him off and attempted to push herself up, but immediately fell back, cradling her hip in her paw. "Why did you follow me? You should've gone back home!"

"I only did what Grampa would do."

Gran tried to smile. "Thank you, Rory. But we're no closer to him, either. I didn't find out anything from that dormouse. He didn't notice me until there was no time to talk. He seemed pretty useless anyway."

"I could talk to him from this side," said Rory. "There are air holes in the back of his cage, see?" He pointed toward the dormouse's chamber. "If I can get up there, I can call him over." Rory let himself out the cage door.

"Okay, but if someone comes, you hide."

Rory turned back. "I'm not letting you go anywhere alone."

"You may have to," said Gran, trying to push herself up again.

Rory slid down the table leg and crossed back to the opposite wall. It was gypsum and bashed up badly, making it easy to scale. He pulled himself from gash to gash until he reached the canvas and climbed to an air hole. A metal screen behind it twanged quietly as he adjusted his claws and cleared his throat to speak.

"Who's making that *aw*ful racket?" said the dormouse sleepily.

"Over here, sir," called Rory, waving a paw through the air hole.

The dormouse staggered over and stopped close, resting on his haunches. He was much taller than Rory thought.

"And who are *you*?" The dormouse looked down at him with large black eyes.

"My name is Rory and I'm a Weedle—"

"You're a mouse, *ob*viously." The dormouse slumped to one side and rested on an elbow, sighing. "And what's so interesting about that?"

"I'm wondering if you know anything about my grandfather—"

"How would I know anything about *you*? I hardly get out much, as you can see." The dormouse waved his paw around to show the whole of his space.

A human girl appeared at the other side of his chamber and stared through the glass. As soon as the dormouse moved, her face lit up. Rory ducked down.

It was the girl from the toyshop!

He peered back again. The girl yanked on an adult's sleeve and began to talk excitedly. The adult pulled her away, across the room.

"Yes, sir, I can see that you're, um...not free," Rory continued. "But maybe you've heard of a mouse called Willis Stowaway? He's like me, with a furry striped tail." Rory slid his tail through the bars. "Maybe he was at the lab where you come from?"

"Well, *first* of all, innocent little tick, I don't 'come from' a lab. I actually had a life out *there* once, believe it or not." He flicked Rory's tail and it fell outside the bars again. "And secondly, I'm rather tired." The dormouse gave a dramatic yawn and turned away.

"I—I didn't mean to offend you. I just want to know if you've ever met a Weedle Mouse before."

The dormouse looked back. "Funny there should be *two* of you hounding me today. Not often I get visitors—not, at least, of your sort." He stared out the glass again and sighed.

"Please, sir, I need to know quickly," said Rory, eyeing the door to the bird room through the glass. "Or I'll have to ask the mouse next door."

"That busybody hill-builder? You won't get anything out of him. All he does is make mountains out of woodchips." He looked down at Rory. "You seem awfully worried about something. Aren't you a little small to be out alone?"

"I'm with my grandmother, sir. She's trapped in a cage on the table behind me. I've got to find out where my grandfather is so we can leave before the Humans take her away."

The dormouse shifted his weight and chewed purposefully on a claw.

"Yes, I saw her fall. Not that *I* could do anything about it." He licked his paw carefully and sniffed, half-interested. "So what was it you wanted to know again?"

"If you've ever seen a Weedle Mouse like us before? We think my grandfather was caught and taken to the lab where you, er...live, and he might still be there. His sister already escaped, and—"

"Oh, *that* one! All hail the ones who break free!" The dormouse turned and bowed to Aunty Hazel's empty chamber across the room.

"You knew my great-aunt?"

"Well, not personally..."

Rory nodded, waiting.

"Look, if you want to know if your grandfather is at the lab, you'll have to go yourself. I don't meet every mouse there, only the ones in the same *trial* as me."

"Trial?" Rory glanced back at Gran, dropping his voice. "What do they *do* to you?"

The dormouse leaned closer.

"Let's just say we work *hard* for our cheese."

Rory watched the dormouse crawl away. What was he talking about? Rory was about to call out another question, when he saw some movement on the other side of the glass. The little girl was jumping up and down in front of Aunty Hazel's chamber, squealing so loud that he could hear her through the door.

The door!

The guard suddenly came through from the bird room and headed straight for the hidden door. Rory ran back down the wall, hitting the floor so quickly that his legs buckled under him. But in no time he was up and running again. He had to get Gran to safety!

He climbed back up on the table and opened the cage.

"So what did he say?" said Gran, lifting her head.

"We've got to get out of here! The security guard is coming." Rory tried to help her up again, but she wouldn't move.

"My shoulder's broken and there's something wrong with my hip," she groaned. "I can't get up."

Rory's heart sank.

"Go back to Mama and Papa," said Gran, laying her head back down.

"No! I won't leave you."

"Don't worry about me; I won't be alone. They'll take me to the lab and I'll be with your grandfather."

"I'm coming with you. We can all escape together!"

Gran was silent.

"I'm coming with you," Rory repeated firmly.

"What about Mama and Papa?" Gran looked at him squarely.

Rory gulped, realizing this would be an adventure like never before. Would he ever see his parents again? How long would it take them to escape? The dormouse seemed so hopeless, locked up for so long.... Rory looked back toward him, but his eyes stopped at the hidden door.

"I wonder how that key suddenly appeared." The guard's voice boomed as the door swung open.

Rory dived under the woodchips, narrowly missing the light that spilled over the table. He lay unmoving under a single layer of cover.

~

Morgan played Ring-nut by himself in the yard. It was getting dark, and Bimble was already in bed. Miss Creemore was talking to Mama and Papa in the kitchen. He felt totally alone.

If only he'd asked Rory what he and Gran had been talking about in front of the fire the night before. Rory had said he was going to help Gran do something.... Morgan knew it wasn't berry-picking; that had been a lie, he was sure of it now. Then at the table, Gran had winked at Rory...

Morgan began to think he should have been a better listener. Maybe if he had pushed himself harder to care before, he would know where Rory and Gran had gone.

Miss Creemore came outside.

"I'm so sorry about all this, Morgan. Your parents are quite upset. It looks like something might have happened to Rory and your grandmother."

"Well, it's not even dark yet. Maybe they'll still come home." Morgan wasn't familiar with the feeling that squeezed inside his chest. He bit his bottom lip.

Miss Creemore put her paw on his shoulder. "I do hope so."

"What a pickle!" said the curator, examining Gran through the bars. "It's not the same mouse who ran away, but it *is* the same breed!"

"Really?" The guard sounded pleased.

"At least the lab will get the same kind of mouse back, so they shouldn't be too upset. They might actually be excited! Congratulations, Tom. I'll see to it that you get that reward." He patted the guard on the back and opened the cage door. "Oh! The latch wasn't closed. Having a problem with locks today, Tom?" He laughed, then put something inside the cage and secured the latch. "I'll be back tonight to load up the other mice."

The guard scratched his head and rattled the door latch, checking to see that it was locked. "I was sure I closed it...," he mumbled to himself.

Rory pushed back the woodchips as the guard's footsteps faded down the hallway. A water dish and a tray of food pellets sat on the woodchips near Gran. He helped her take a drink, fed her a pellet of food, and then put one in his mouth.

"Yuck!" He spat it out. It was nothing like he'd tasted before—an unrecognizable, perfectly round piece of—what? Gran had a similar reaction, but with the unknown looming before them and their pouches left behind, they ate the next ones quietly.

Rory felt the pellets move dryly down his throat. While the strange food seemed to fill his stomach with lead, his mind filled with questions. How far were they going? How would they escape? Would Gran get better? And would anyone come looking for them? Mama and Papa might assume they were dead, like Grampa. But what about Morgan?

The only comforting thought was that they were drawing closer to his grandfather. He smiled at Gran, who patted his leg in return. She soon fell asleep, eerily silent without her usual snores. Rory hid back under the woodchips to rest for the journey ahead. He didn't know how they would ever get home again, but at least he knew they'd be with Grampa.

∾

Morgan stayed outside to watch the moon rise. Mama and Papa hadn't seemed to notice it was past his bedtime. He wanted to go in and talk to them, but he didn't know what to say. He couldn't tell them that he thought Rory and Gran might actually be alive. What did he *really* know? Nothing. And he didn't want to get their hopes up, anyway.

Morgan suddenly realized he had wandered off their hill and followed the moon up the old streambed to the farm. He passed under the fence and crawled across the empty pasture to the road. All was completely quiet, not a bird or mammal in sight.

He sat by the recycling bin, hoping a bulldozer would come by. Maybe if he could get back into town, he could look for them himself. But no vehicle of any kind passed. If only he'd taken that bicycle from the toyshop, then he could go anywhere he liked.

❧

After a few hours, Rory felt the cage lift, swaying in time with the smack of shoes against the floor as they traveled down a maze of echoing hallways. A moment of quiet passed before a heavy door clanged open. The smell of fresh night air wafted through the cage. The curator said a few words to someone and then another door slid up. The cage was pushed along a metal floor until it hit a wall. Rory counted nine more cages as they scraped across the floor to join them. He poked his head out of the woodchips, but the cage was covered in a blanket and he couldn't see anything. He hid back under and waited.

An engine choked into life and Rory felt the vibrations of a van pulse through his fur. The cage shifted slightly as the engine roared ahead. A sharp turn made him lurch into a puddle where the water dish had spilled. He crawled out of the wet woodchips and felt for Gran in the dark. She hadn't moved; she still lay on her side. He nuzzled in beside her belly, taking care not to lean on her bad arm.

He lay awake for a long time, too excited to relax. All he could think about was meeting his grandfather again. He could hardly believe how close it was to reality.

The engine whined continuously. It was hard to know how much time had passed or how far they had gone. He wondered if the lab was in Seekum, or some other town. Maybe it was in the World Beyond. If it was a place where Humans put the mice to work, like the dormouse said, he understood why Papa refused to take them. He hoped Mama wouldn't worry too much.

At last the engine stopped. A beam of light flashed through the blanket, falling for a moment on Rory's face. He hid himself quickly.

"One, two, three…," a voice counted as the light moved over the cages. "…Nine. Where's the tenth?"

"They're all there. Loaded them myself," said the driver.

"Okay—I see it. Will you help me take them inside?"

Rory felt the cages drag across the floor. Gran woke and lifted her head.

"Where are we?" she croaked, half awake.

"I think we're at the lab," said Rory, his voice muffled by the woodchips.

Theirs was the last cage to be taken inside the building, which hummed with fluorescent bulbs. After a few turns down a hallway, Rory felt the cage set down. The lights went out as he heard the gentle click of a door closing. He listened to footsteps fade down the hall before he poked his head up and sniffed, surprised not to smell the other mice nearby. In fact, the only scent he could pick up was one he hadn't smelled before. It pierced his nose, like the stench of rotten egg. He clawed at the blanket through the bars until it slid off the cage.

They were alone in a small, white room. The cage sat on a counter next to a sink, with cupboards above and below. An empty table sat along one wall, and the other walls were lined with tall shelves holding various shapes he couldn't identify in the dark. A blue night-light met with the yellow beam of a streetlight that shone through a high window, combining into a sickly patch of color on the floor.

Gran stirred feebly. Rory helped her take the last drop of water from the dish before she nodded off again. His own eyes soon became heavy, and he hid himself under the woodchips, taking care to cover his ears and tail properly. It was up to him to figure out how they would escape, and he couldn't do that if he was discovered. Tomorrow he would find out where the rest of the rare mice had been taken; that would surely lead him to Grampa.

And then they would all escape together.

THE MOUSE IN THE MACHINE

Morning arrived with a loud bang. For a moment, Rory forgot where he was and thought a pot had fallen to the floor at Glasfryn. But one sniff of the air brought it all back.

A Human was forcing a lever lock to bang open on the window overhead. The bustle of heavy traffic grew louder as the window cranked open. Rory pushed his ears up to listen. It didn't sound like Eekum-Seekum out there. With a gentle press on his shoulder, Gran warned him to stay low.

A second Human entered the room. "Morning, Lee. I see you're already armed and ready." The man laughed as the sound of someone putting on latex gloves snapped through the air.

"Yup. The museum curator was right—it's the same breed, all right, but she's injured. We'll have to work quickly before the bones heal improperly." The woman's voice was gentle.

"Okay, let's get her into surgery."

Rory's heart skipped as the cage door rattled open and a hand reached inside. Gran squeaked as the man pinched the base of her tail and slid his fingers under her belly.

"*Gran!*" Rory whispered from under the woodchips.

"It's okay," whispered Gran as she swept over Rory in the palm of the man's hand. "They're going to help me."

"I see she's got a dislocated shoulder," said the man.

"And her left hip looks odd too," said the woman.

"Let's clean her up."

The pungent scent Rory had picked up the night before grew stronger. After a few moments the door opened and shut again, and all was quiet. He lifted his head to look out. He could see a closed jar and some used tissues on the table where they must have washed Gran in the smelly liquid. As he stared at the table, he suddenly realized that his view was clear of bars—the cage door was open! Now was his chance.

With no pouch to carry food, he quickly stuffed some pellets in his cheeks and crawled out of the cage to look for a new spot to hide. It had to be near enough to Gran to watch over her but far enough away to stay out of sight.

A cord hung down from the cupboard above and plugged into an outlet by the sink. He climbed up the cord and found a radio at the end of it, sitting on top of the cupboard.

Rory considered as he bit on his claw. He could hide behind this machine, whatever it was. He was high up, directly above Gran, with a good view of the room. He spat out the pellets and slid back down the cord, scanning the room for supplies. The shelves were jammed with boxes of scissors, tissues, swabs, and rubber gloves. He ran across the sink and jumped onto the table, climbed down a leg and onto the bottom shelf, where he snatched some cotton balls and carried them back up to his hideout. He shredded them into a comfortable bed, imagining a peaceful sleep without Morgan to steal the blankets for once. Oh—a blanket. He ran back down to the counter and began to gnaw through the blanket that had covered the cage. He needed only a small square, but it was going to take some time to chew through whatever kind of fibre it was; it tasted like plastic. He hid himself in the folds and set to work.

After a while, the Humans came back. Rory crept along the counter underneath the blanket and hid behind a roll of paper towels, then peered around to watch. The man was carrying Gran on a tiny stretcher.

"Well, that went all right," he said. "Won't be long before she's healed."

"Hard to say," said the woman. "She's older than other mice we've operated on. It could take longer for her to heal from a broken hip."

The man lay Gran on the table. Her mouth was open and her tongue was hanging out, spilling drool.

"It's a pity she's not the one that escaped," said the woman. "We won't be able to finish our study now." She gently closed Gran's mouth.

"But it's fantastic that another one turned up! We can begin a new study. Maybe she'll yield new results. Let's measure her while she's unconscious."

Rory began to feel queasy as the Humans prodded Gran, counting the stripes on her tail and measuring the circumference of her ears.

When they were finished, the woman lifted Gran gently and put her back inside the cage. She refilled the food dish and attached a water bottle to the bars, handing the old water dish to the man before she latched the door shut. The man put the dish in the sink and turned the tap on, peeling off his rubber gloves. He washed his hands and then reached for the paper towel.

Rory shrank back as a finger nearly grazed his whisker.

The man dried his hands and patted the cage. "Get well soon," he said.

"I'll check on her later," said the woman. And they left.

Rory came out from hiding and hurried to the cage. A sling held Gran's arm in place, and her hip was shaved bald, revealing a row of stitches. The Humans were certainly taking care of her. Could this place really be as bad as the dormouse said?

Gran was sound asleep, so Rory decided to explore. He finished chewing off a square of blanket, and brought it up to his hideout, before looking around again. Then he saw it—an air vent in the wall near the ceiling. What luck! He could explore safely that way, just like the street drains in Eekum. He slipped through the grating and made his way along the metal duct, memorizing his route. Right, left, up, down. Each time he arrived at a new vent, he popped his head out to look.

The first vent looked down on a long white hallway with several doors leading off on each side. The second led to a washroom.

The third vent opened on an enormous room filled with rows of open-shelf units on wheels. The shelves were crammed with milky-white plastic bins. Overhead, air hissed through large orange pipes.

As he scanned the room, Rory thought he saw something move inside a bin on one of the shelves. He leapt out of the vent, dashed across the concrete floor, and hopped onto the shelf. When he put his eye up to the plastic bin, he could see what had moved inside—a white mouse with black patches and bright pink eyes. Rory waved but the mouse only hunched down and stared at him. He was about to question the mouse about Grampa, when the shelf suddenly jolted.

Rory poked his head out from behind the bin only to quickly draw it back in. A Human was wheeling the shelf unit down the aisle.

A door banged open into a stark, white room. The Human pushed the shelves through and joined three other Humans in white lab coats behind a long counter. "These are albino mice, in day six after undergoing gene therapy to restore pigmentation," he said. "Any changes in fur color must be recorded by digital photo and uploaded onto the network computer." He slid the cages off the shelf one at a time and passed them to the other Humans.

The shelves emptied quickly. With lightning speed, Rory jumped off the unit and disappeared down another vent, where he stopped to take a breath. There were hundreds of shelves with thousands of bins in that room—and there might be many more rooms just like it. How would he ever find Grampa?

The next vent led to a smaller, carpeted room. There were no cages anywhere, just a strange flat box on a desk in front of a chair. Rory had never seen a computer before. He climbed up the chair.

The desk was covered with papers and a mess of cords. Lying in front of the strange box was a long rectangle with squares lined up in rows on it. On most of the squares was a letter or number but Rory couldn't make sense of it. What did *QWERTY* mean? Maybe he could read the papers.

He leapt toward the desk but the chair swivelled as he jumped and he fell onto the keyboard. To his surprise, the squares pushed inward and a sharp bleep rang out as the computer screen flashed and lit up. Startled, Rory jumped up and fell onto a plastic oval with a long cord attached to it, like a tail. There were more *bleeps* as the video of a mouse began to play.

"H-Hello?" said Rory. The mouse didn't reply. It looked extremely old—it was pale and hairless, and covered with waves of deep wrinkles. It scratched its ear with a paw, which emerged from a thick fold of skin.

The mouse turned in a circle, crawled straight ahead, and stopped at a wall. The camera pulled back.

Rory watched in confusion as the mouse grew smaller and a maze of walls filled the screen. Was the mouse inside an Amazer game? He moved closer and knocked on the screen.

"Can you hear me?" The mouse looked as puzzled as he was. Rory noticed some words written along the top of the screen.

File. View. Table. Window. Help.

That was strange—was the mouse asking him for help? Rory looked at the keyboard again, wondering if he could spell out a message in return, but then he saw the arrow keys. He could direct the mouse out of the maze! He pushed excitedly on the Up key.

An arrow appeared on the screen but the mouse went in the opposite direction. Rory yelled, "Go up! UP!" and pushed the arrow again. The mouse moved left, the camera following it toward a bit of cheese. The mouse ate it hungrily, then continued left. Rory hit the Up key furiously. "No, it's a dead end! You can't get out that way!"

A hand appeared on the screen and replaced the cheese. Rory jumped back. Where did that Human come from? He looked around the room but no one was there.

His eyes fell back on the keyboard. There had to be *some* way to communicate with this mouse. He wished Morgan was with him; he was brilliant with the Amazer and would know exactly how to help the mouse escape. Rory's mouth fell open as he spotted a button that read *esc*. Did that mean escape? Could it really be that easy?

He ran across the keyboard, stepping on a number of keys as he went. He hit the *esc* button and looked up, but the mouse and the maze were gone. Text and charts had taken their place.

Rhino, read Rory. *Lab mouse showing signs of premature aging. Room 11, bin 2318.* He thought about what the dormouse had said—"We work hard for our cheese." This mouse must be *really* overworked!

As he ran back down the chair, Rory wondered if Gran was under good care after all.

When Rory returned to his hideout, he found the woman had come back already. "So how are we doing?" she said.

Rory heard the cage door rattle open below and he peered down carefully. The Human was talking to Gran.

"In a month or two, you'll be good as new," she said.

A month or *two*? Rory's eyes grew wide.

"You'll be ready to roll."

Ready for what? Were they going to put Gran in one of those mazes too?

"I've got a treat for you," said the woman, and she reached up to the top of the cupboard. Rory drew in a breath as he dashed behind the radio. If his hideout was discovered, he'd be in trouble—the Humans would set traps everywhere.

"This will keep you company," said the woman. She turned the radio on and soft music filled the air.

Rory sighed in relief as the woman moved her hand away from his hideout. She locked the cage and left the room. He climbed down to the counter.

"Gran, you're awake!"

"H'lo Rorily," said Gran in a garbled voice. "Did you fly away?"

"I went exploring." He began to lift the latch on the door.

"No! Stay underground. The falcon will return." Gran didn't make much sense but he decided not to upset her. Instead, he put his paw through the bars and stroked her ear.

"How do you feel?"

"Light as air."

"Are the Humans being nice to you?"

"They're fairies."

"What?"

"Mouse doctors."

"Humans have doctors just for mice?" Rory was confused.

Gran looked at him. "Where are your wings?" She stretched out her good limbs and flapped them. "*I'm a fairy grandmother*," she sang.

"What are you talking about?"

"I'm tired," she said, curling into a ball.

"Okay, you sleep."

"Did you find anything in the forest?"

"I didn't find Grampa yet, if that's what you mean."

Gran grew still.

"But I will," he said firmly. Her eyes blinked heavily and she fell asleep. He climbed up to his hideout, the sound of the music growing louder in his ears. Taking some food from his stash, he fell into bed, munching slowly. Would he really be able to find Grampa in this enormous place?

Rory watched the grass tremble in the breeze outside the window. A goldfinch pecked at the ground, its feathers ruffling softly. It was a refreshing view after the stark walls of the lab. The bed seemed to grow softer and Rory dozed off.

When he woke again, the music had stopped, replaced by the sound of a Human voice. Rory froze. He peered out from his hideout but he could see no one. As he crawled to the edge of the cupboard to look down, the voice suddenly moved behind him. He spun back around, expecting to see someone in the window, when he suddenly laughed at himself. It was the radio.

"And now, the news in brief," said the voice. "The mayor urges all residents of Grule and surrounding towns to prepare for multiple hurricane threats this season after a report was published yesterday—"

Grule! So they *were* in the World Beyond! He thought back to the map on the wall at Glasfryn. How far beyond its border they were, he could only imagine. With any luck, he'd find Grampa soon and get them home before Terrible Things happened.

Night fell. The sallow glow from the streetlight began to fill the room. Rory sat up to look for the moon, but he couldn't see the sky over the tall buildings. He could hear Gran's voice in his head: "Looks like it vanishes completely, doesn't it? But it's always there, Rory. It's always there."

He lay back and closed his eyes. Even if he couldn't see how to find Grampa now, the answer would show itself eventually. At least he had some time to search before Gran healed and the Humans put her to work. They would have to escape before that.

Morgan turned over in bed, unused to the space without Rory there. He pulled the blanket higher and tried to sleep again but he couldn't relax. Rory and Gran had been missing for a whole day now, and everyone was losing hope they'd return. If only he could find them somehow.

He slipped out of bed and crept to the kitchen pantry, where he lit a candle to look for a snack.

The shelves were neatly packed with boxes of Juneberry paste that his parents had spent the whole day organizing. He had begun to ask if they could go back to Eekum to look for Rory and Gran that morning, but Papa had cut him off. After his parents discovered he'd wandered out to the road by himself the night before, Morgan was banned from going anywhere for the rest of the summer. His parents were really upset with him, even though they must have known how scared he was feeling too. Didn't anybody care how he felt?

Morgan watched the candle flame squirm on the wick. He wondered if Rory ran away on purpose. If that was the case, then he kind of understood.

❦

Rory ate breakfast slowly. He'd had yet another night of sleep disturbed by dreams of going home and finding no one there. He'd lost count of how many weeks had gone by. He tried not to think of his family. How many more days would go by before he'd see them again?

"So where will you explore today?" asked Gran, passing him another pellet through the bars.

"Er...there are two rooms I haven't searched yet," he replied, pushing the food through his teeth.

"Good, so we'll find your grandfather soon," said Gran.

Rory tried to smile but it came out like a wince. He had actually been through the entire lab six or seven times by now and had searched every bin, nook, and cranny. Not a single mouse had spoken to him, let alone offered any information. They were all busy working for the Humans, it seemed, and had forgotten what it was to be free. The pressure was mounting to get out of there, fast. Soon he would have to tell Gran the truth—that they would have to leave without Grampa.

"I'm feeling much better these days," continued Gran, "I'm ready to go home." She hummed along with the music on the radio.

Gran was indeed more energetic than ever. The Humans had put a wheel in her cage and she ran on it every day. Her shoulder was back to normal and the fur was growing back on her hip. But Rory was exhausted.

"What's the matter with you?" teased Gran, pinching his cheek. "Your old granny can run twenty minutes straight and you can barely feed yourself!"

The music stopped and a human voice began to speak. Rory pretended to listen, avoiding his grandmother's question. He was used to the bodiless voice on the radio now and remembered how it startled him the first time he'd heard it. It reminded him of the wrinkly mouse in the maze on that first day of exploring, before he knew what a computer was. Only then, he could see the mouse but couldn't hear it....

Rory spat out his food. That was the answer! "You look like you spotted an owl!" said Gran.

"Uh, yeah. I've got to go—day's wasting."

"Well, drink some water first." She turned the spout toward him.

Rory slurped some water down and wiped his mouth.

"See you later!"

He ran up the radio cord and slipped through the vent.

"Be careful!" Gran yelled after him but he was already running at top speed down the air duct. His face drew back in a smile—he *finally* knew where to look.

Rory had spent a lot of time watching the Humans when there was nowhere left to explore. He would spy on them through the air vents, hoping one of them would say something about where the rare mice were kept. But all they talked about was their experiments, like the one they were doing with the wrinkly mouse. The Humans were getting excited about how it was progressing. They were constantly in front of their computer screens, tap-tap-tapping on those things they called keyboards, recording their research. He couldn't believe he hadn't thought of this before—of course there would be something on the computer about Grampa too! He ran faster.

At the fifth vent, Rory climbed out into a quiet room with only one desk and a computer on it. He could hear human voices that came from the kitchen nearby. He would have to hurry.

He jumped onto the keyboard and pressed random buttons until the screen lit up. Words appeared at the top, the same as he had seen on that first day, only they made sense to him now—*File. View. Table...*

Beside the keyboard sat the plastic oval with the long cord attached. At least there was one "mouse" that could help him. Rory watched the screen as he dragged the mouse across the desktop, searching for an arrow that moved in sync with the mouse. He pushed it to the left and back a bit, and the arrow landed on *File*.

He pressed the button on the mouse and a list of new words appeared. *Open. Save. Print...*

Rory moved the arrow to *Open* and clicked the button again. A long list of files filled the screen. He scanned down the list and there it was: a file entitled "Rare Mice." Hooray! He clicked on the file name and the screen filled with tiny images of all the mice he'd seen at the museum. He moved the arrow and clicked on Aunty Hazel's image.

Specimen ES-1. Long-tailed field mouse of unknown origin... He didn't need to read that again. At the bottom of the screen, two words were underlined: *Similar specimens*. He pulled the mouse toward him and clicked on the words.

The screen filled with a giant image of Grampa. Rory's heart flipped but he read on, steadily.

Specimen ES-2. Trapped with ES-1. Routine studies have not yet revealed where these mice originate. They eat anything, though at times have shown preference to berries indigenous to the Weedle River region. Specimens show an unusual ability to solve problems and a keen interest in obstacle courses, breaking all previous records held by other species. However, they are unpredictable and distinctly hostile, often chewing through maze walls. In fact, their behavior is so erratic that in some cases researchers could only conclude that they are capable of forethought and manipulation, resulting in botched testing and periods of what can only be labelled as hunger strikes. Hence technicians were not entirely surprised that both specimens escaped—

Both escaped?

Rory choked. He stumbled and hit the button on the mouse, causing the screen to change. An image of Gran appeared, looming over him. How was he going to tell her that Grampa had gone? If he escaped with Aunty Hazel and only *she* made it home...

Morgan was right after all. Grampa was dead.

Rory sat back on his haunches. He couldn't believe the journey would end like this.

"Gotcha!"

A human voice boomed as a white cone came down over him. Rory curled into a ball and closed his eyes.

ᦡ FOURTEEN ᦢ

AWAKENINGS

Morgan lifted the cellar hatch. The morning sun cut through the dust in the hollowed-out hole below. He crawled down the ladder headfirst.

The cellar was covered in piles of scavenged junk—bits of rubber and wire, elastic bands, and string. Plastic spoons and straws hung on the wall, and bolts of scrap fabric rolled on toothpicks were stacked on a shelf. Morgan shuffled through the piles, looking for a sharp nail.

Bimble's old play-tent lay folded on the floor. He lifted it up, hoping to find the nails he'd used as tent pegs. Instead, he found a kite Rory had tried to make out of a silver-dollar plant's seedpod. As he picked it up to blow the dust off, his claw tore the membrane and ruined it. He sighed and put it down carefully at the foot of Gran's cat-tickler, which leaned against the wall. On the floor nearby was a nail. He tested the tip with his paw. It was perfect for drilling.

The bicycle he was making had only a front wheel so far—a green plastic button with a corrugated edge, great for traction. The back wheel would be a quarter. He'd figured out a way to bow-drill a hole through the middle of the coin by harnessing a nail in the string of a bow, and pulling on the bow ends fast enough to spin the nail, drilling it down through the metal. He'd dulled a few nails already and just needed a final one to finish.

Since the family adventures had been put on hold, there wasn't much else for Morgan to do. His parents spent all their time scavenging and hoarding, and Bimble wasn't interested in playing with him anymore. All she did was draw and write on any scrap of paper she could find—preparing for school, Morgan assumed. Nobody talked about Rory and Gran. And since Morgan had exhausted every possible idea about where they might have gone, all he could do was keep busy too. Hope was a distant feeling.

The cellar grew suddenly dark.

"There you are!" cried Mama, looming over the hatch. She sounded relieved, but looked angry. "I've been searching for you! I need you to tighten the wheel on the wheelbarrow. We're taking Bimble to the farm."

Morgan climbed up the ladder to the yard. It wasn't the place it used to be. Grass grew over the Ring-nut pit and the lounge chairs were stacked to the side to make room for the wheelbarrow, which parked near the door. At least the sundial was still there—the last reminder of Grampa, now that Rory and Gran were gone. Morgan leaned over to check the hour, but the gnomon claw left no shadow.

A drop of water fell on his cheek and he looked up to see dark clouds blowing in. He fixed the wheelbarrow and went back to his bike.

Papa opened the door, and Bimble ran out and hopped into the wheelbarrow. A tiny pouch was wrapped around her middle.

"Can I ride?" she said. Papa nodded, smiling. Bimble had grown over the summer; she no longer rode on his back.

"I don't know where you plan to go on that thing," said Papa, eyeing Morgan's bike.

"I have to get it to *work* first," said Morgan, back at the bow-drill.

Papa looked about to suggest something, but then stopped himself. "Well. You know you're still grounded till school begins."

Morgan didn't say anything. When were his parents ever going to be nice again? He felt like he had to be the perfect son now that Rory was gone.

He watched his parents take Bimble down the hill, then finished drilling through the coin. He attached it to his bike, greased the chain with some slime off a rotten pumpkin seed, and wired an acorn shell to the front as a basket. With a cautious paw, he tested the pedals.

"Yesss!" Morgan laughed, amazed that it worked. Climbing carefully onto the rubber seat, he rode around the sundial. "I've finally done it, Ro—!" He caught himself before he called his brother's name.

Now that the bike was working, it was time to test it. "The only thing to do when you're sad is to go on an adventure"—that was

Grampa's motto. Morgan was tired of Papa's rules; from now on, he'd do what Grampa would do.

Morgan raced down the hill, yelling into the wind. It felt good to ride free. He flew into the bog, the bike wheels tearing through the sandy gravel. Maybe he could find that bog pool where Rory saw Mack and Jack on their boat....

"Whoooa, young friend!" A wing came down and blocked him. "You're heading for the mud."

"Oh! Mr. Glee." Morgan skidded to a stop. "I'm not Rory, if that's who you thought I was again. He's missing."

Glee chuckled. "I hope you're looking for him this time."

"It's not like that. He's been missing a long time. My grand-mother, too."

"Oh—I'm sorry. That's terrible."

"My parents think they were killed by a cat." Morgan looked down at his feet.

"Seems as if you don't agree." Glee cocked his head to one side.

Morgan spun a pedal with his foot. He didn't reply.

Glee looked at his bike with admiration. "Nice work."

"Thanks," said Morgan, with a half-smile.

Glee paused, then spoke slowly. "Perhaps the doubt in your heart is a message from your *brain*."

Morgan felt the urge to protest, but Glee spoke again quickly.

"Well, you look like you're having fun, so..." He turned to fly away. "Take care to know where you're going!"

Morgan watched him fly off. *Stupid bird*, he thought. *Of course I know where I'm going*. He carried on, to look for Mack and Jack.

The gravel soon disappeared into mud, under a thicket of cranberry bushes. Glee's warning passed through his mind, but Morgan jumped off his bike anyway, and led it under the branches.

The wheels of his bike soon began to sink. He was struggling to lift his bike out of the muck when he heard a voice over the rising wind. No—two voices. He yanked his bike out of the mud and ran to the edge of the bushes. But when he saw Mack and Jack on the boat, he suddenly felt self-conscious. Ever since word got out that Rory and Gran were lost—in town of all places—the Stowaways had been shunned. Mack and Jack probably wouldn't even talk to him.

Morgan put the bike down and hid behind a rock. Maybe he could learn how to sail by watching.

The boat was keeled over to one side, and the sail was luffing wildly in the mounting wind. Jack turned the wheel round and round, but the boat wouldn't change direction.

"Where are you going?" Mack yelled. "You're heading for shore!"

Jack shouted back, "I can't help it if the boat won't turn!"

"You were supposed to fix the tear in the sail! And now we're going to *craaaaaash*!"

The boat rammed into shore, directly in front of Morgan. Mack pitched forward over the rail and landed ears-first in the mud. Morgan turned to scramble under the bushes, but it was too late. Mack saw him.

"What are you looking at?"

"Nothing," said Morgan.

"Good, then go away." Mack wiped the mud off his drooping ears.

Morgan turned his head to leave but he just couldn't lose his chance. "Will you teach me how to sail?" he said.

"Not likely, short stuff," grunted Mack. "We've run aground." The boat had tipped so far over that the sail nearly sagged in the mud.

"I could help you," said Morgan, hopefully.

Mack scratched his armpit as he eyed the bike. "You make that?"

Morgan nodded, feeling confident again. "I'll fix your sail if you give me a lift across the pond—I'm kind of stuck here." He pointed at the mud caked on his wheels.

"You'd let a *Stowaway* on our boat?" said Jack as he clung to the mast.

"Well," sniffed Mack, "we need some extra paws. At least he's not as scrawny as his brother was."

Morgan clenched his teeth. He didn't like Mack talking as if Rory was dead. Well—*he'd* prove the Stowaways weren't easily defeated. He strode into the bushes, came back out with a reed in his paw, and tore it into thin strips. Then he climbed onto the tilted deck and up along the mast. He caught the flapping sail in his paws and poked two rows of holes along the tear with his claws. Threading the reed through the holes, he sewed the tear closed and tied knots at both ends. He climbed back down to shore, nodded at Mack, and together they pushed the hull upright. The boat loosed from the mud and slid back into the water.

The wind immediately picked up the sail and the boat began to drift away.

"Hold close!" yelled Mack. Jack struggled at the wheel to keep the boat alongshore. Morgan grabbed his bike and held it over his head as he and Mack waded through the water toward the boat. Mack lifted the bike on deck and Morgan pulled himself up under the rail.

Jack gave him a nod. "I guess you weirdos are good for something."

Mack laughed.

"*Now* will you teach me how to sail?" said Morgan with a cheeky smile.

"Hah! Okay. But you have to keep working." Mack pointed to a rope attached to the sail. "You take the halyard and do what I tell you. Jack, stay on the wheel."

With much grunting from Jack and yelling from Mack, they journeyed across the great pool. Morgan grinned from ear to ear as the wind blew over his fur like grass in an open field. He focused on the sail, doing exactly as Mack instructed. Though the boat leaned heavily to one side, they kept it on course and finally reached the shore on the opposite side.

Mack thumped Morgan on the back as Jack guided the boat alongshore. "You sailed like one of us."

"Thanks!" Morgan splashed into the shallow water below. "That was even more fun than I thought!"

Mack passed the bike down to him. "You'll have to teach me how to ride this thing next time."

Morgan smiled widely and waded to shore. As he waved good-bye, he was overcome with emotion. He had finally proven the Stowaways' worth to another Weedle Mouse—and there was no one to share it with. His parents were too busy to care, Gran was gone, and Rory... He wiped a tear away and headed home, skirting the bog this time.

When he arrived, Miss Creemore was waiting in the yard, pacing back and forth.

"Oh—hi, Morgan." Miss Creemore forced a smile. "What are you up to?"

"Nothing much." Morgan jumped off his bike and leaned it against the sundial.

Miss Creemore looked at it curiously. "That reminds me of some-thing your aunt—" She stopped herself.

"Who?"

"Oh, er, I meant *Miss Bucket*. Your bicycle reminds me of a story *Miss Bucket* told about the old days.... You know."

Morgan shrugged. Miss Creemore was acting weird.

"Where are your parents?"

"Out scavenging, as usual."

"Tell them I'll come back later, all right? There's something urgent I must speak to them about."

Morgan watched her hurry down the hill. What was all that about? Adults were so tiresome with all their hidden meanings. He went inside the house to lie down and marvel over his fantastic day. He scurried toward his bed.

"Ow!"

Something poked out from under the sack of feathers. Bimble must have hidden his Amazer. He caught the edge with his claw and pulled it out, but it wasn't his game—it was Rory's book from the market. Wasn't this what Rory and Gran had been poring over the night before they disappeared? A page fluttered to the floor and he picked it up.

"The Proud Mouse and The Trap." He read it aloud.

Morgan lay back on the bed as his mind filled with questions. Was this story about a *Weedle* mouse? Is that why Rory and Gran thought it was so important? He tried going over all the facts about their disappearance again, but still, nothing made sense.

His parents finally believed that Gran and Rory were eaten by the toyshop cat, but that didn't seem right to Morgan—Gran wouldn't have let that happen. And now he was beginning to understand why Rory doubted Grampa could be killed in a trap. There *had* to be another explanation—his grandparents were too feisty to let themselves meet such fatal ends.

If only he'd insisted Rory tell him what was going on that night before their last adventure. But he knew it was an empty wish—when it came to his brother, he'd never been a good listener.

Morgan bit on his claw as he thought of what Glee said earlier. If doubt was a "*message* from his brain," then maybe Rory and Gran *were* still alive. But what could he do about it, when even his parents couldn't do anything?

He looked out the open door at his bike leaning against the sundial, and suddenly stood up. He could go sleuthing on his own, now! The first thing he would find out was what Miss Creemore was covering up. Every time she mentioned Miss Bucket, she acted strange. One of them knew something—and Miss Creemore wasn't talking.

He looked at the map, found Miss Bucket's name by the cliff, and threw the book into the basket on his bike. "Take care to know where you're going," Glee had said. Well, he wasn't entirely sure yet, but Morgan was certain he'd be back before his parents even knew he was gone.

❧

Fallen leaves curled in mini tornadoes under the willow trees, as Morgan rode in the mist along the bank. Once he reached the cliff, he put the bike down and looked over the edge to the beach below.

The slope was awfully steep to crawl down. He sniffed along until he found a small vent-hole that emitted the smell of smoke. There must be a mouse-hole below. He leaned over the edge again and saw a little staircase, switch-backing down the cliff.

Morgan left his bike behind and carried the book in his tail as he crawled carefully down the stairs. Maybe Miss Bucket could explain how the book might be important.

The stairs stopped at a rock plateau, at the entrance to a tunnel. He sniffed inside. What was that awful smell? Staying close to the wall, he crept slowly down the tunnel. It seemed to wind on forever until he finally saw light from the crack around a door. A terrible stench was coming from it—the smell of burning fur!

Morgan pulled the door open.

"Cursed ravens!" An ancient mouse was hunched over a bedside table, cradling one paw with the other, the fur singed and smoking. The candle beside her had fallen over, and the wick was still lit, carrying the flame precariously close to the bed. Morgan ran over and smacked the book on it.

"Aah!" screeched the old mouse. "Where did you come from?"

"Sorry, I didn't mean to scare you," said Morgan, squinting. The room had gone dim. A single lantern was left alight at the far end of the room. Miss Bucket wasn't anywhere around. "Who are you?"

The old mouse glared. "I might ask you the same!"

"I'm Morgan Stowaway. I live on the other side of the bog."

"Well!" The old mouse softened. "You're a timely acquaintance." She cracked a smile before her forehead wrinkled in confusion.

As she moved back into bed, Morgan saw she had no tail. There was something oddly familiar about that—Bimble used to babble about a mouse with no tail. He'd assumed it was just one of Gran's stories.

"Who are you?" Morgan repeated.

"Pardon me?" said the old mouse, nestling under the covers.

"Who ARE you?" Morgan leaned into her ear.

The old mouse seemed too confused to answer. Morgan began to feel frustrated. According to the map, Miss Bucket was supposed to live here, not this crazy mouse. He wrenched the book out of the cooled wax and turned to go.

"A book!" said the old mouse, surprised. "Give that here."

Morgan reluctantly passed it to her.

"I used to read these in the city."

"Oh, yeah?" said Morgan in disbelief. Only his familiy had traveled outside Biggle's farm.

"Oh, yes. There were thousands of books in Grule."

"Grule?" Stunned, Morgan sat down on a stool. "In the World Beyond? *You've* been there?"

"Don't sass me, crumpet. I am a Stowaway, after all."

"No you're not," Morgan snorted. "I just told you *I* am. That's why you said it. You have no idea who you are." He put his paw out to take the book back.

"Hang on," said the mouse, keeping hold on the book. "I'll have you know that me and Willis went farther than any other mouse in the history of Weedle River!"

"My *grandfather* Willis? How do you know him?" Morgan froze.

"He's my brother."

"*You're* Aunty Hazel?" Morgan stood up. "But Gran said you're dead!"

"Well if I'm dead, then so are you!" she said, cackling.

"Papa said you were caught in a trap." Morgan felt a chill go up his spine.

"Well, now you're talking sense. That's true...." Aunty Hazel sat upright, with a sobering look on her face. "What is this place, anyway?" She looked past him.

Morgan ignored her and flipped the book to the loose page, pushing it back under her nose. "Do you know who this story is about?"

Aunty Hazel picked up the page, her face turning solemn as she read. "Not *exactly* how it happened..." Aunty Hazel scratched her head. "But this story is *definitely* about your grandfather."

Morgan's jaw dropped open. "My father said he was killed!"

"No," said Aunty Hazel quietly. "At least, not then."

Morgan fell back on the stool. "W-what happened?"

Aunty Hazel settled back on her pillow and drew her paws into her lap. She was about to speak when Miss Bucket appeared in the doorway.

"Morgan!" She ran straight toward him. "You're not supposed to be here!"

"Is she really my great-aunt?" he asked.

Miss Bucket shook the mist off her fur and sighed. "Yes."

"I remember everything, now," said Aunty Hazel, looking at Morgan. "You were a baby the last time I saw you. You've grown so much."

Miss Bucket sat on the bed, her mouth hung open in shock—finally, Aunty Hazel's mind had cleared.

"Your grandfather and I were trapped by Humans at the museum in Seekum and taken away to a lab," continued Aunty Hazel. "I don't know where it was, or how long we were there. Often, we were in darkness. New mice arrived; other mice went. Time no longer mattered. The Humans put us through maze after maze, offering us food from every forest they could think of, trying to find where we came from. But we never gave them a clue.

"Then one day, I overheard a Human say we'd be part of an exhibition of rare mice at The Museum of Natural Curiosity—the very place where we were abducted. In one week, we'd be close enough to home to give us hope! They only planned to take me, since I was in better shape than your grandfather. But he was determined to go too. At the earliest chance, he turned on one of the Humans and bit her while she was cleaning his cage out. Your grandfather escaped and pretended to run away, but the next day he hid inside my cage under the woodchips, waiting for moving day.

"But this story is definitely about your grandfather."

"At the museum, your grandfather slipped out of the cage while they were transferring me to a glass chamber. I don't know where he hid himself. All day, visitor after visitor streamed by my chamber. I remember one particular girl who kept coming back, staring at me with her greedy little eyes. It was terrible—far worse than at the lab, where at least we had some privacy.

"By night, your grandfather chewed on the screen behind my chamber. After three nights, he finally opened a hole big enough for me to get out. It took us until morning to find a door that led outside; we'd forgotten what open air smelled like. We ran for our lives, knowing the Humans would be after us by then. But your grandfather was weak from his efforts to free me. He strained to keep up, and in my haste I didn't look back for him often enough. Somewhere along the alley behind the toyshop, he vanished."

Morgan stood up, his heart racing.

"I looked everywhere, but there wasn't so much as a squeak from him to guide me." A teardrop ran down her whisker. "That's when I was attacked. A cat pounced on me and tore off my tail. The pain was terrible, but at least I got away. I ran and ran and ran." Aunty Hazel closed her eyes. "I don't remember anything after that."

Miss Bucket took her paw to comfort her.

"How long has she been here?" Morgan asked quickly.

"Miss Creemore found her a week or so before Rory and Gussie went miss—"

Before Miss Bucket could finish, Morgan bolted for the door. "Where are you going?"

"I've got to hurry." He slipped out the door.

"Why? What's wrong?" Miss Bucket called after him.

Morgan's reply echoed down the tunnel. "Nothing!"

This time, he knew *exactly* where he was going.

"I know where to find Grampa!"

✑ FIFTEEN ✑

HOME AND AWAY

The cold grid of metal sank into his fur as Rory slumped against the cage bars. A tear ran down his nose and fell on his tail, which lay like limp string at his feet. He lifted it up to count the rings—ten blurry stripes and a new one had begun to darken. Gran said the stripes grew in with every stage of wisdom, but he sure didn't feel any wiser. Not only had he failed to find Grampa, but he had gotten himself trapped. And now he and Gran were doomed to be lab mice, never to return home.

Outside a tree blew in the wind, its branches rapping eerily on the window like tiny knuckles begging to be let inside. Rain began to splatter against the glass.

Rory looked out at the brewing storm. A streetlight flickered on behind the swaying tree, but the fractured light would never be enough to see the other mice in the room. All their cages, including his, were lined up in cubbyholes along one wall. He could only smell their presence.

✑ 177 ✑

He curled into a ball, tucked his nose under his paws, and tried to sleep. He would give anything to be squished in bed beside Morgan again.

"Aha!" said a voice.

Rory jumped up. Was he dreaming?

"Gran! How did—"

"That Human chatterbox who comes to check on me just couldn't keep quiet. Great grackles, she talks a lot! 'We found another like you,' she said. Hah! If Humans knew we understood them, what a different world it would be. She even told me where they put you—in the rare mice room on the fourth floor."

"What? But I searched every room in the building!" Rory was amazed.

"We're in the building next door. There's a link between the two, on the top floor."

Rory smacked his forehead but knew it didn't matter, anyway. Grampa was dead. And he wasn't looking forward to telling Gran.

"But how did you escape?" he asked.

Gran smiled. "I can make friends with birds too," she said as she opened the door of his cage.

Rory stepped out. "They keep birds in here too?"

"No. The Human left the window open and a goldfinch hopped inside," said Gran. "She spotted your nest and wanted to take it. I thought it was you rustling around up there, so I called out. I must have scared the wits out of her because she fell on top of my cage! She was about to fly off but I begged her to stay. I told her our story and said that you were suddenly missing and I was left with no hope of escape."

"So she let you out?"

"She was reminded of her brother, who was caught and kept in a cage. She felt sorry for us. So, yes, she did."

Rory was overjoyed. "Let's go home!" He turned to run.

"Just a minute—we have to find your grandfather first," said Gran.

He stopped cold.

Gran's whiskers twitched. "What's wrong?"

Rory hesitated. "Just before they trapped me, I found a research file on Grampa." He lowered his head. "He escaped with Aunty Hazel."

Gran frowned. "Nonsense! How could Hazel have made it home and not him?"

Rory could hear her teeth grinding. "I don't know, but—"

"Exactly!" cut in Gran. "You don't know anything."

"But I looked through every room."

"Well, you never found *this* room, did you? He's probably right here!" Gran scurried along the shelf to check each cage in its cubbyhole.

Rory sighed. It was true they had finally found the place where Aunty Hazel and Grampa were kept all that time, but he knew it was no use. "I can't imagine either of them leaving the other one behind," he called after her. "Can you?"

Gran reached the last cubbyhole and stopped, her shoulders hunching sadly. Rory gave her time to grieve. He had been forced to accept reality for some time, but to Gran it was new. Grampa was really gone.

Gran returned, picking at her claws with her teeth. "Hmpf," she grunted.

"I'm sorry." Rory tried to take one of her paws but she jerked it away.

"Fine, fine. Let's just get out of here, shall we?" Gran pushed past him and scuttled back along the shelf. "Any of you geniuses know how to get to Eekum-Seekum?" she yelled.

"Gran, shh!" Rory pulled her back. She was really upset.

"Well, they've been in this place for an eternity; they must have heard *some*thing, don't you think? Or do *you* have some fantastic plan to get us home?"

A familiar voice rang out. "Who's making that awful racket?"

"None of your business!" cried Gran.

"Gran!" Rory scolded, then replied to the voice himself. "It's Rory Stowaway. Who's there?"

"Ha, ha! We meet again!"

A gust of wind blew the tree outside, and the streetlight flashed across the room. The dormouse was in the cage right beside them, leaning casually against the bars.

"Oh, terrific," said Gran dryly. "It's the *dumbmouse* who got us into this mess."

"Hello, sir." Rory greeted him politely.

"I see you brought your grandmother a long way for nothing," said the dormouse, looking down at him.

"*You're* the one who led us to this dead end!" said Gran.

"Oh, no, no, I didn't lead you anywhere. You heard what you wanted to hear."

"Oh, really?" Gran curled her paws into fists.

Rory nudged her and she reluctantly stepped aside. "Sir, we really want to go home now. Do you know how to get to Eekum-Seekum?"

The dormouse looked disappointed that the sparring match with Gran was over. "Why should I help you again? I might *lead* you astray."

"If you help us, we can help you too," said Rory.

The dormouse fell silent. Gran snorted.

"Don't you want to escape?" said Rory.

The dormouse slipped back into shadow.

Gran waved her paw to dismiss him. "Forget it, Rory. He's too much like the other mice here. He's forgotten what it is to be free."

The dormouse stepped forward again. He gulped. "I—I guess I never thought it could happen."

"Well, now's your chance!" said Rory. "You can go home."

The dormouse paused. "I have no home to go to."

"Come with us," said Rory.

Gran made a sour face. "Huh!"

"Really?" said the dormouse.

"Sure, why not?" Rory knew he was getting somewhere; the dormouse was biting.

"Well, there is one way to get to Eekum-Seekum, but I can't guarantee it. Open my cage and I'll show you."

Rory moved to unlatch the door.

"Oh, no, no." Gran pushed him aside and poked her claw through the cage bars. "You tell us first, and *then* we'll let you out. You'd probably run off without us."

Rory wished Gran would stop arguing. It was getting late, and a Human would come by on rounds soon.

"Fair enough," said the dormouse. "There's a van that comes every night to collect the mail from the box in the parking lot."

Rory unlatched the door.

"Wait," said Gran, holding the cage door shut. "Are you suggesting we mail ourselves home?"

"That is correct." The dormouse pushed the door open and stepped outside. "Free!" he said, spinning merrily then bowing low to Gran. "Rénaud le Souris at your service, Madame!"

She frowned at him. "All right, all right, you've had your moment. Now, let's go!" Gran ran toward the window, unlatching the rest of the cages as she went. "At least it gives them the option," she said with a shrug.

When no other mice appeared, she jumped on the window ledge. Rory and Rénaud followed behind.

"You mean to go this way, Madame?"

"Call me Gussie," said Gran. "And yes, I mean to go this way. It's the fastest way down. Didn't you say the mail truck comes soon?"

Rory pressed his face against the rain-spattered glass. He could just make out the puddles on the ground, far below.

"Forgive me for sounding obvious," said Rénaud, "but wouldn't we die if we jumped?"

"We *climb* down." Gran took hold of the crank, and Rénaud and Rory helped her open the window. They pushed it up and pulled it down until the frame opened with a loud *crack*. A strong gust of wind nearly knocked Rory over, but Rénaud held him up.

"It's wild out there!" Gran yelled over the storm. "Willis would have loved this." She crawled through the opening and onto the ledge outside. Rory and Rénaud followed as the tree's swaying branches threatened to swipe them off their feet with one spontaneous blow.

"Do we climb down the tree?" said Rénaud, squinting through the driving rain.

"Too dangerous!" yelled Gran. "There's only one way." She pointed to a drainpipe bolted to the stone wall more than a yard away from the window.

"That looks awfully slippery," said Rénaud.

"Exactly!" said Gran.

Rory knew better than to argue. Once she made her mind up, that was it. Gran jumped on and slid down, out of sight within seconds. Rénaud moved to the edge to watch. He looked back at Rory, gave him a crooked smile, and jumped.

A roof gutter snapped overhead in the wind. Rory looked up as a spout of water poured through the crack. He backed up to gather his courage. He couldn't wait much longer—

"Ow!"

A Human had grabbed his tail. Rory fell forward and clutched at the ledge as the Human tried to drag him back inside.

"Noooo!" The Human's fingers slipped off his wet tail.

There was a crash above as the gutter split in half and a curtain of water began to fall. Rory scrambled up and leapt onto the drain-pipe. He closed his eyes in terror as the water gushed around him, filling his ears and nostrils.

He had to let go, or drown.

︎◦◦᷎

The mud crammed under Morgan's claws as he climbed the stairs. He'd stayed a long time at Miss Bucket's; it was getting dark outside and the mist had turned to rain.

Morgan couldn't understand it—why had Papa kept Aunty Hazel a secret? Morgan had always supported his father, assuming he knew best, even though his rules were sometimes harsh. But he couldn't believe Papa would choose to keep him from the truth—danger, maybe, but not the truth.

He turned up the next flight of stairs. So Rory and Gran *had* run away on purpose, to find Grampa. Now he understood what Gran's wink had meant the night before their last adventure—she and Rory had been planning to search the museum. But they wouldn't have found Grampa there, Morgan knew. He hoped they hadn't met a terrible fate instead...

He wasn't sure how to find Rory and Gran yet, but he knew he could still save Grampa—as long as his bike could take him there.

But when he reached the top of the cliff, he discovered it was gone.

"Ha-ha!" Tamrin taunted him as she ran away with his bike toward Biggle's fence.

"Hey!" Morgan skidded after her. The rain was falling steadily now and the grass was soaking wet. "Give it back!"

"Make me!" Tamrin stopped and sat on the bike seat, trying to figure out the pedals. The second she stepped on one, the bike lurched forward and fell. Morgan ran up to her.

"Please give it back. I've got to go somewhere, fast."

"Where?"

"None of your business. And it's *my* bike." He grabbed it from her.

"Hey—I wasn't done with it!" Tamrin pulled it back, but Morgan wouldn't let go.

"It's mine," he said firmly.

"Mine!"

"Squawk!" Glee flew down beside them and landed close to Tamrin. She screamed and ran away.

"Good riddance!" Morgan called after her. He turned to Glee. "And good timing. Thanks."

"You look like you're on your way somewhere."

Morgan checked the bike for damage. "I'm going to find my grandfather, and hopefully Rory too."

A gust of wind ruffled Glee's feathers. "Shouldn't you tell your parents first? Maybe they can help."

Morgan caught sight of Miss Bucket running along the cliff. He was sure she was going to tell Papa Aunty Hazel's story. But what would Papa do about it? Probably nothing, as always. All he cared about was rules and boundaries and staying safe. But those things wouldn't help anyone now.

"I can't wait anymore." Morgan adjusted the chain on his bike and jumped on the seat. "I'm going to Eekum."

Glee put his wing against the handlebars. "A storm is pushing in from the east, exactly where you're headed."

Morgan pushed through his wing and rode under Biggle's fence. "It's okay—I know where I'm going now!"

"Please reconsider!" warned Glee.

Morgan looked back as Glee flew off toward Glasfryn. He was probably going to warn Papa. Morgan pedaled faster; he didn't want to be caught. But as he coasted down the driveway, past the petting zoo and out to the open road, he felt doubt slow him down.

Could he really make it all on his own?

❧

Rory clamped his eyes shut as he was swept down the waterfall, heading for the ground. He braced himself for impact, but it never came. An arm reached out to grab him.

"Phew! That was close." Rénaud held him by the scruff of the neck until Rory clawed at the stone wall and found his grip. "We have to climb down the wall now. Can you do it?"

Rory nodded, glad to be alive. The stone was slippery and it was a sheer drop two floors down, but there was no other way. Taking their time to get their footing, they carefully scratched their way down to the ground.

Gran was waiting for them. She grabbed Rory and squeezed him tight, then turned to Rénaud and murmured, "Thank you."

Rory coughed up water before he was finally able to speak. "The Humans—they're after us!"

Gran looked alarmed. "Where do we go?"

"To the mailbox!" Rénaud took the lead as they scurried along the foot of the building.

The clouds had darkened into a haunting shade of green. Rory shivered as the wind swept through his drenched fur. He followed

Rénaud to the parking lot and under a white van. Was it the same one that had brought them here, and his grandfather before them? Sadness welled up inside him again. He wished they were leaving with Grampa. But there wasn't time to grieve.

"RUN!"

Lights flickered on over the parking lot, flooding it like a sports field. The basement door sprang open and a string of Humans ran out in yellow raincoats with flashlights in their hands, chasing several mice. The other rare mice must have run! Rory spotted the mailbox on the other side of the lot. He and Gran dashed across, hidden in the splashing rain.

"Rénaud's too big—they'll see him!" shouted Rory, looking back. Rénaud had fallen behind, wobbling like a young racoon pushing through the wind. The Humans scanned the ground chaotically with their flashlights, nets ready in their hands. Rory and Gran reached the mailbox and hid underneath.

Rénaud dodged a beam of light as he scuttled under a parked car. The Humans gathered back together at the far side of the lot, then formed into a line. They slowly scanned the ground, covering every inch as they moved toward the mailbox. Gran waved frantically at Rénaud to run. He finally staggered to shelter.

"I'm no runner," he gasped. "Climbing is more my thing."

"That's fortunate," said Gran, sticking her head up inside a hole at one corner. "Because we have to climb up here. I think it leads up to the mail chute." Her voice echoed inside the hole.

"How will I fit in *there*?" said Rénaud.

"You'll have to suck in your tummy," said Gran, pulling her head out again.

"Isn't it slippery?" said Rory, knocking on the metal.

"We can cling to the rust. You first." Gran hoisted him up. "Quick! They're getting close."

It was pitch black inside the hole. Rory tested the rust on the walls and climbed all the way up, crawling inside the mail chute at the top. Gran arrived shortly after, shoving her head back down the hole to look for Rénaud. "I hope he can fit through."

"Hello." Gran flinched in surprise. Rénaud was only an inch from the top. "I'm stuck," he said flatly.

The sound of Humans shouting suddenly thundered through the mailbox.

"I saw one go under there!" yelled one of them.

"Open it up and look!" cried another.

"Help me pull him," said Gran. Rory tugged at one ear while Gran yanked on the other until finally Rénaud came up, coated in rust. They were about to jump from the chute into the mailbag below when they were jolted back. A Human had pulled on the handle and tilted the chute out into the storm. Rain slapped at the metal as they scrambled up the slope, dodging the flashlight.

"There they are!"

"It's the stripe-tails!"

"Get them!"

"Jump!" Gran leapt over the edge of the chute and down to the mailbag. Rory and Rénaud tumbled in after her as an engine rumbled outside. The mail van had arrived.

"Perfect timing!" shouted a Human, slamming the chute back in place. A door slid open on the van. "The mailman will get them out."

Rory cringed. They were trapped!

"Evenin'," said the mailman suspiciously. "What are you all doing here?"

"Well, uh…we've lost some mice down the mailbox." The Humans laughed nervously.

Rory held his breath as the mailman rattled his key in the lock and opened the door to the mailbag. The wind blew inside, crumpling the canvas around him.

"Sorry—can't help you," said the mailman. "It's a federal offense to tamper with the mail. Once it's gone, it's gone."

Rory let out his breath, smiling. They were safe!

The mailman carried the bag to the van, while the Humans followed, begging him to open it.

"NO!" said the mailman. "This mail is going to the depot, where it will be weighed, stamped, sorted, and stacked like every other bag of mail. And there is nothing you can do about it!" He threw the bag into the van and slammed the door shut.

Rory's stomach lurched as the bag slid to a halt on the floor and the mail tumbled forward around him. By the sound of it, they weren't quite safe, yet.

Morgan steered around the puddles of rain in the road. It would take hours to get to Eekum on his bike. As he passed Biggle's farm, he could see that the windows and doors were nailed shut with planks of wood. There wouldn't be any vehicle to catch a ride on tonight—the Humans had all taken cover from the coming storm.

He looked across the dark pasture toward home. Glasfryn would be dry and safe. But home didn't feel like shelter anymore; it felt empty to Morgan. His parents were heartbroken—even he could see that. He sped up. At least he would bring Grampa home tonight!

Crunch! Morgan hit a pebble and flew over the handlebars. His front wheel fell off and rolled down the road and into the ditch. He stumbled to the edge just as it floated away down a stream of rainwater.

Morgan sighed heavily and considered going home again. But there was nothing for him there but Papa's anger. He looked down the road ahead. If Rory and Gran could do it, so could he. He left his bike where it was and pushed on through the wind, crawling down the highway.

It was going to be a long night.

ᴥ SIXTEEN ᴥ

BITTERSWEET REUNIONS

Whoosh! Rory fell down amidst boxes and envelopes as the mailbag was emptied into a huge rolling drum. He clawed at the air but there was nothing to cling to; everything was falling— and everyone.

Gran and Rénaud shot past him, their weight propeling them down. Rénaud hit bottom first and slid straight through with the boxes while Gran careened to the right with the padded envelopes. Rory was thrown left with the regular letters.

The drum spit Rory onto a conveyor belt that immediately swept him up a steep incline. Before he could catch his balance, he was dodging the beaters of a machine that smacked the envelopes around him. He had only a split second to save himself before being bludgeoned.

He dived between the beaters and fell down to another conveyor belt, which whipped him to the right this time and straight across an enormous room lit with thousands of lights. Rory put his paw over his eyes to shield them from the glare.

"Gran!" He spotted her on a roller belt as she sped past him in the opposite direction. She was clawing at an envelope, trying to stay upright as it flew over the rollers.

"Don't juuuump!" Her voice sounded distorted as she zoomed by. Rory only heard, "Juuuump!"

He leapt onto the roller belt to follow her, his legs nearly slipping through the rollers. Pitching back and forth, he found his balance by running on the spot like a logroller on a river. He could hardly believe how bad their luck had become—it would be a miracle if they got out of there alive.

Up ahead, Gran was speeding toward a machine with a slotted face like a pastry cutter. Bubble wrap popped as the padded envelopes squeezed through in front of her. Behind her, Rory leapt onto a passing packet and immediately whizzed toward her.

"Jump off, Gran!"

"Too laaaate!"

She was sucked between the slots—and a half-second later, so was he. His ears flipped inside out as he was forced through the narrow space. Inside the machine, the belt suddenly slowed and jerked forward.

Rory popped his head over the edge of his slot and shook his ears out. Gran was in the next slot, up ahead. He jumped over and squeezed up the aisle toward her.

"I'm okay, I'm okay!" said Gran, sitting up. She shook out her whiskers, which were bent like an accordion.

Rory closed his eyes as they passed a rapid flashing light. As the belt sped up again, the smell of ink grew strong in his nose. What was coming *now*? He dropped down and stretched out, hoping to miss the next machine (whatever it was), when something flat punched his stomach. He gasped for breath as the belt came to an end and dumped him over the edge and into a hamper. Envelopes fell all around him. He felt like throwing up.

"You okay?" Gran was right beside him.

"I guess so," said Rory, rubbing his belly. Gran moved his paw away and pointed at his stomach, smiling. He looked down at himself and grinned. "Eekum" was stamped across his belly.

"Hey—look!" Rory and Gran ducked down at the sound of a Human voice close by. "This photo came out of the coding machine. We have an intruder!"

Rory peered through a hole in the hamper. The Human was holding an image of Rénaud, flattened against the camera lens with his paws splayed over his eyes.

"Oh, this explains the call I just got." Another Human had entered the room. "A scientist from Grule is looking for some lab mice that escaped in a mailbag."

"Hah! That was no scientist—it's Joe, pulling pranks again; I bet he slipped this photo in the pile and then snuck out to call you."

"That rascal—imagine us looking through this entire place for a mouse!"

The Humans burst out laughing and walked away.

Rory and Gran poked their heads out over the envelopes. Rénaud's head popped up from the hamper next to them, his black eyes swirling in the fluorescent light. Rory read the label on his hamper: "Rejects."

Everyone laughed, relieved that they were finally going home.

Dong. Dong.

The bell of a clock tower rang faintly over the sound of the engine. Rory's ears perked up as he woke.

"Did you hear that?" he said.

Gran stirred in the mailbag nearby.

Dong. Dong.

Rory sat up. "It sounds like the museum clock in Seekum."

"So we made it, then!" said Rénaud, pushing aside an envelope.

"No thanks to you," said Gran sleepily.

Dong. Dong.

"I beg your pardon, Madame!" said Rénaud, with a hearty laugh. "I believe I got us this far."

"We were almost *squashed* in that mailroom," mumbled Gran.

"Well, we're safe now," said Rénaud.

Dong. Dong.

"Eight," said Rory over the last sounding bell.

Gran looked irritated. "Eight what?"

"It's eight o'clock."

"I hate that bell. It sounds like doom." Gran sighed.

Rory understood her pain. The last time they had both seen Grampa was underneath that very clock tower. He wished with all his heart that things had turned out differently. He took Gran's paw to comfort her, but they were suddenly thrown forward. The mail van had stopped.

The door slid open. Rory felt the mailman drag the bag toward him and lift it onto his shoulder.

"I *had* to choose the job that never cancels due to weather," grumbled the mailman.

Rory climbed over the envelopes and poked his head out from under the flap. Twigs and leaves blew past his nose in the rain. Though it was morning now, it was still nearly dark as night. The mailman headed toward an old green door with a tarnished brass mail slot. Rory's heart leapt; it was Sparkle's Toyshop!

The Human's hand brushed past him as it dug inside the bag and grabbed a large manila envelope, bending it in half.

"Eek!" Gran squealed—she was caught inside the fold. Rénaud squeezed in after her and Rory grabbed for his tail, just as the mailman pulled the envelope out of the bag.

Rory hung off the edge by a claw, in full view.

"What the heck?" The mailman shook the envelope violently. Rory fell, but the wind blew him sideways into the mailman's leg. He scrambled down the Human's uniform and ran under the toyshop door, where he waited anxiously for Gran and Rénaud.

The brass flap opened and the wind whistled through. The corner of the envelope appeared but then stopped, stuck. Rory cringed as it wiggled and crumpled in the slot, then finally hurtled through and dropped to the floor.

"Ouf!" said Rénaud, shaking his head. "Did my brain come out my ears?"

"Don't be silly!" said Gran. "That was only a bit of trouble."

Rénaud winked at Rory. "Glad to see you here."

Rory smiled back at him, relieved they made it through.

"In all my adventures," continued Gran, "That would rate as maybe a level two challenge."

"Level two? Out of how many levels—two?" said Rénaud, supressing a smile.

"My husband's narrow escape from a falcon would rate as a level ten."

"Well, I don't think I've missed out by not experiencing a level ten, then." Rénaud chuckled.

"No, I don't imagine a wimp like you would appreciate it. My grandson, on the other hand, enjoys a little adventure, don't you?" Gran patted Rory on the head and he smiled distantly, looking toward the back room of the toyshop. What was that flapping sound?

"Shouldn't an *adventure* be quite different from a near-death experience?" Rénaud smiled.

"Only if your idea of adventure is eating your food from the opposite side of the bowl," said Gran. "Right, Rory?"

She looked around, surprised. "*Rory?*"

™

The cat flap fluttered noisily as Morgan pushed through to the back room of the toyshop. He didn't think he would ever come here again.

The room still hadn't been tidied. The pile of green water pistols was gone, but stacks of boxes still littered the place. He rounded a corner and froze. A tower of cat-food tins stood at the base of the staircase. He only hoped the beast had already eaten. He crept on silently, with the eerie sensation that something was watching him.

"Morgan?"

He spun around.

"Rory!"

The brothers threw their arms around each other, laughing ecstatically.

Morgan pulled away at last. "Why does your stomach say 'Eekum'?"

"We came with the mail!" Rory giggled, brushing a paw through the ink on his belly. "But why are *you* here?"

"I'm looking for Grampa—did you already find him?"

"Grampa? No." Rory wrinkled his brow in confusion. "You and Papa were right all along. He's not coming home."

"No, no! *You* were right. Aunty Hazel—"

"You know about her?"

"Yeah, I found her at Miss Bucket's yesterday. She told me everything that happened to her and Grampa."

"She did?" said Rory. "But she lost her mind!"

"I know she's a little nuts, but I showed her that book of yours and it seemed to snap her out of it."

Rory closed his eyes and sighed. "We were going to do that too. But then Mama announced we were going on an adventure to the museum the next day, and we decided not to wait for Aunty Hazel's memory to come back."

"Is that why you and Gran left us? To look for Grampa at the museum?"

Rory looked down at his feet. "I'm sorry—I should have told you what was going on. After everything that happened at the toyshop, we knew Papa wouldn't let us go there, so we had to go on our own."

"I know. And I don't blame you. I'm the one who should have listened more. If it makes you feel any better, I messed up too."

"How?"

"I came here on my own and I didn't tell Mama and Papa either."

"At least we'll be grounded together this time," said Rory.

Morgan grinned.

"So, did Aunty Hazel tell you how Grampa died?" Rory asked, though he wasn't looking forward to the answer.

"No! That's why I'm here. He might be *alive!*"

Rory gasped.

"Aunty Hazel said Grampa escaped the museum with her, but when they ran away, she lost him. Here, Ror!"

"*Here?*"

"Yes! In the alley out back. She thought it was a cat that got him, since it attacked her too. But I don't think it was the cat…."

"What do you mean?" Rory was incredulous.

"Remember when we were here last and that Human tried to catch us? Well, I guess you got away quickly, but that girl meant business—she was really after me! So when Aunty Hazel told me a particular girl kept coming back to see her at the museum—"

"I saw her there too—"

"It led me here." Morgan looked intently at his brother.

Rory's eyes grew wide. "The *girl* caught him!" He turned toward the shop. "I'll get Rénaud and Gran—we've got to search upstairs."

"Who's Rénaud?"

Rory was about to answer when Morgan pushed him hard.

"Watch out!" he yelled.

A Siamese cat burst through the flap and pounced on the spot where Rory had been standing.

"Run high!" Morgan bolted up a pile of boxes, his claws piercing the cardboard in a trail of holes. Rory tried to follow, but the cat leapt up and knocked him with its paw.

"Nooooo!"

Rory slammed down on the floor. The cat hunched over him and hissed, its teeth glazed with saliva.

Morgan jumped down and stood between the cat and his brother, puffing out his fur. He swiped at the cat's face, his claws ripping through the air. The cat reared back, exposing its fangs with delight as it lunged forward. Morgan thought it would be the last thing he ever saw—

"Get out of the way!" A heavy paw gripped his shoulder and hurled him to the floor. He looked up and saw a strange creature jump onto the cat's face and claw its cheeks. What was *that* thing?

The cat threw its paws up, yowling.

"Quick—help me." Gran tapped Morgan on the shoulder and they dragged Rory behind the stack of boxes, out of sight. Gran checked his pulse; he was alive but unconscious.

Morgan peered back around the corner. The creature was holding itself like a muzzle over the cat's jaw.

"Who *is* that?" he said. "*What* is that?"

"Rénaud le Souris," said Gran. "He's a dormouse."

"Can he win against a cat?" asked Morgan, doubtfully.

"Let's hope so."

"*Rowrrr!*" The cat fought fiercely as the dormouse kept hold on its face. Fur fell in clumps on the floor as it tore at Rénaud's back.

"I've got to help him!" Morgan ran toward the cat before Gran could stop him. He leapt onto its neck and pulled hard on its ear. The cat let go of Rénaud and swiped at Morgan as it shook its head wildly. Rénaud fell hard on the ground. Gran ran past him and leapt toward the cat, but it lunged at her first and knocked her back to the floor. Morgan ran down the cat's spine and slid down its tail, yanking on it hard. The cat turned quickly on him and was about to pounce, when a gust of wind blew the cat flap open.

The cat and Morgan watched in surprise as a wet, brown mouse dropped to the floor.

"*Papa*?"

The cat licked its lips at the larger mouse. Morgan rolled out of the way and joined Gran and Rénaud, where they watched from behind the beast.

Slowly, silently, Papa advanced. He looked huge with his fur stuck straight out—almost as big as the dormouse. Rénaud got up and snuck quietly behind the cat, so now he and Papa cornered the beast from both ends. They were all about to pounce, when heavy shoes began to clack down the stairs.

Morgan looked up in dread as the light flicked on.

"Fluf-fy! Break-fast!" It was the human girl.

The cat turned toward her as she hopped down the last few steps, carrying a bowl of cat food.

Papa took his chance to dash across to Gran. He and Morgan

helped her to safety behind the box, where Rory was still unconscious.

But Rénaud was caught between the cat and the girl. When she reached the last step and saw the dormouse, she screamed. The bowl of cat food dropped on his head.

Morgan peered around the box. Rénaud was knocked out, covered in smelly tuna.

"What are *you*?" said the girl, gazing down at the strange creature. The cat didn't dare make a move toward the dormouse—it looked quite as afraid of the girl as Morgan.

Slowly, silently, Papa advanced.

Gran raced toward Rénaud. "We've got to save him!"

"Mother—noooo!" Papa ran after her.

The girl squealed. "It's the mice with the funny tails!" She disappeared into the shop, leaving Papa and Gran to swiftly drag Rénaud behind the box. But with the girl now gone, the cat came back to its senses and began to sniff hungrily along the trail of tuna left by the dormouse.

The girl returned quickly. Morgan didn't think he'd ever be so happy to see her again—the cat seemed to freeze in her presence. She had a net in one hand and a wet manila envelope in the other.

"My nature magazine!" She put the net down, sat on the bottom stair, and ripped it open. "*Finally!*"

"Mary! Breakfast!" A voice came down the stairs.

"I'm not hungry!" said the girl, flipping through the pages.

"Now or never!" said a louder voice.

The girl closed the magazine and glanced at the net, pouting. Terrified, Morgan watched her climb the stairs. As soon as she was gone, the cat advanced toward them again, a watery growl building in its throat as it neared their hiding place. Morgan shook Rénaud and he got up, stumbling.

"We've got to get out of here," said Papa. He lifted Rory in his arms.

"I'll lead the cat away," said Rénaud. "If I go with you, he'll only find us again. I stink of fish."

"Sounds like a plan," said Papa, turning to run. Gran looked unsure, but there was no time to think.

"Wait—we've got to go upstairs!" said Morgan, tugging at Papa's arm.

"What? No way. We're going home," said Papa.

"But Grampa's up there!"

"WHAT?" Gran clutched Morgan's shoulders. "What do you mean?"

"Rory and I figured it out. She's got him up there!"

"Who?"

"That human girl!"

Papa's mouth dropped open.

Rory came to, rubbing the bump on his head. "What's going on?" he said groggily, as Papa let him down.

"We're going upstairs to find your grandfather," said Gran. She grabbed Rory's paw and pulled him toward the stairs, directing Rénaud as she went. "We'll meet you outside, friend. Good luck."

Rénaud ran out in front of the cat, drawing it toward the back door as he yelled back at Papa.

"*Go!*"

Papa stood still, a look of deep shock on his face.

At the top of the stairs, Rory's senses returned as he crept behind Morgan and Gran. The sour smell of moldy wood filled his nostrils and his head was throbbing. He wasn't quite sure what had happened downstairs—was that really Papa?

He slowed down as another, deeper scent took him over. His heart jumped.

"Smells like something sweet rotting, doesn't it?" said Morgan, with his nose upturned. "Apples?"

Rory passed in front of him. "We have to hurry," he said. The peculiar smell grew stronger as they crept down the hallway.

"The Humans are eating a meal," said Morgan.

"No, that's not it…" Rory couldn't find the words to tell his brother.

Gran sniffed the air and nodded. "You're right—there isn't much time."

Light from the kitchen flooded across the hallway as they reached the first doorway. Rory motioned to Morgan and Gran to stop, as he peered into the room.

"I saw more of those special mice again," said the girl, swinging her feet under her chair.

"There are no special mice, Mary," her mother sighed. "It's all in your head."

"You never let me have any fun," whined the girl.

"Your 'special mouse' is a *hamster*."

Rory looked back at Morgan. A hamster! Were they wrong?

"Well he's mine, and I want another one!" The girl slammed her fork down and crossed her arms.

"Sit up and eat your eggs," said a growling voice. The girl's father grabbed her chair, dragging it toward the table as it screeched across the floor.

Rory waved to Morgan and Gran—now was their chance to cross the doorway unnoticed.

They scampered across the light and down the dark hall. The second door led to a bathroom, the third to a bedroom. The fourth was a living room, where the television was on with no sound. The last door was closed.

"In here," said Rory, sniffing under the crack and squeezing through.

The streetlight swayed in the wind outside the window, casting a dim, uncertain light across the girl's bedroom. Toys were strewn across a flower-shaped rug, which lay under a pink bed and a white desk and chair.

"Up there," said Rory. He wove his way through a pile of dolls and scrambled up the chair to the desktop, where he stopped in awe.

Covering almost the entire surface was an enormous cage—but it wasn't scary like the ones he had come to know. It was beautiful. Branches of silver birch hung with pressed orange leaves were tied to the bars like the walls of a forest. Elaborate tunnels of cardboard tubes towered to the top, where the ceiling was lined in paper, painted blue with cotton-ball clouds. Golden boxes filled with fresh flowers nestled among the woodchips. Something stirred inside a wooden box lined with moss.

Gran pushed past her grandsons. "Willis?" she said quietly, fumbling with the latch. Morgan helped her lift the metal catch and she crawled inside, Rory at her heels.

"Gussie." A scratchy voice answered his grandmother. Rory felt a lump move into his throat.

Gran crawled inside the box, curled up beside her husband, and put her arms around his neck. Rory and Morgan followed, nestling in beside their grandparents. Grampa was breathing softly but unsteadily. As he exhaled, Rory recognized the peculiar scent again, though it was much stronger now.

It was the smell of life fading.

"You found me." Grampa moved a paw to stroke Gran, but he had only the strength to touch her face. "And you brought my little boys." He looked at Rory and Morgan, a smile flashing over his cloudy eyes. "All grown up."

Rory and Morgan stared back at their grandfather. He was just a wisp of the mouse they imagined.

"They're like you. Determined." Gran's voice cracked as she spoke.

"Hi," said Rory quietly. He felt shy in Grampa's presence.

"I always believed you were alive," continued Gran, "but I lost hope, too many times."

Grampa wheezed through his reply. "My memories of you...kept me alive."

"Dad!" Papa ran across the woodchips.

"Him too?" said Grampa, craning his neck slightly.

"I never—I didn't think—you're alive!" Papa fumbled over his words.

"Shh. It's okay; it's almost over now." Gran reached for her son's paw. Papa crouched down at his father's side, his eyes watering. He hardly recognized the old mouse—his fur was mottled white and his belly was almost bare.

Grampa lifted the end of his tail and Papa took it in his paw, shaking as he spoke. "You left us behind and I—I missed you so much, Dad. I blamed you for choosing adventure over us. I didn't know how wrong I was, until now. Forgive me."

"There's nothing to forgive," said Grampa. "You had a family to care for. You did the right thing."

Papa let a tear fall as he looked at his own sons. Rory looked scared. Morgan was angry.

"You kept us from finding him! How could you?" he spat out.

"I didn't mean to—," began Papa.

"Shh," said Grampa, looking at his grandsons. "Don't feel bad." He continued slowly, pausing often. "I was weak…too weak to make it home. The Human girl saved me…from the cat. Look at… my palace here."

His surroundings were certainly more than comfortable, Rory thought. He exchanged a look with Morgan. Though they both felt deeply dissatisfied with their father, they knew Grampa's time was running out, and it was not the time to argue.

Grampa sighed happily. "My last wish…was to see you all. And it came true."

From then on, no one spoke, though the air was moist with joy and pain. The only sound was the wind that shook the window like a passing train. Rory kept his eyes on Grampa and smiled as much as he could, knowing that his grandfather wasn't coming home. Grampa squeezed Rory's paw, then his head fell toward Gran. A wince passed over his cheeks and disappeared, leaving a peaceful stillness on his face.

"He's gone," whispered Gran.

Papa closed his father's eyes.

❧

"You can't make me eat!"

Rory sat up quickly. The girl was coming down the hall.

Papa grabbed Morgan and ran for the cage door, with Gran and Rory following. They slipped through and slammed the latch behind them, then dashed down the desk leg and under the bed.

Soft light fell across the floor as the bedroom door opened and the girl walked quietly toward the cage. The Stowaways dashed out the door behind her, but Rory held back. He watched her lift the latch on the cage as a green pea fell from her hand.

"Breakfast time, Mr. Mouse," she whispered sweetly.

Rory's eyes filled with tears as he watched her put the peas in an empty bowl. Then he turned to catch up with his family.

✿✿ SEVENTEEN ✿✿

HURRICANE GLASFRYN

S irens wailed in the distance as the Stowaways tumbled out the cat flap and headed down the alley. The storm still raged, and the sky was ominously dark. Heavy rain churned through flooded ruts in the asphalt, garbage bins rolled across their path, and bits of sodden cardboard lay everywhere. But there was no sign of the dormouse. Rory's stomach grew tight.

"We can't leave without Rénaud!" he yelled. "He wouldn't leave without *us*!"

Everybody stopped. Papa hesitated, looking at Gran. "I think the cat must have got him, Rory," she said.

"He wouldn't let himself get caught. Not so soon after being freed," said Rory, his paws clenched. Morgan nodded fiercely.

Papa sighed and led everyone out of the rain underneath a garbage bin lid. He sensed Rory was talking about more than Rénaud.

"I really let you both down, didn't I?" he said.

The boys were silent.

"I'm sorry I didn't have more faith in Grampa. I should've let go of my anger a long time ago and searched for him and Aunty Hazel myself. I was just so determined to keep you all home and safe—I couldn't bear to lose anyone else after losing him. Rory, I'm indebted to you for staying with Gran and keeping her safe. Morgan, I didn't see how capable you are. I'm a proud father."

"And Grampa was proud too. Of all of you. I know it." Gran took Papa's paw and squeezed it. Papa gathered his mother and the boys in his arms and they held each other for a long while. Rory closed his eyes, thankful for their last moment with Grampa.

"And what about Rénaud?" he pulled away.

"I'm afraid there's just no hope," said Gran. "He was covered in tuna. That brute was bound to get him."

"But—" Rory trembled. The wind caught the bin lid and it flew up overhead. Everyone watched as it sailed back down the alley, dropping with a clatter against the toyshop door. And that's when they saw him limping along the wall.

"Rénaud!" cried Rory.

The dormouse was alive, but the cat was close behind, stalking him.

"Stay here." Papa ran off like a shot and headed directly for the cat. The cat stopped in its tracks, backed up, and yowled. At the last second, Papa made a sharp turn and dived for Rénaud. He hoisted himself under Rénaud's arm and they moved together, dashing under the bin lid. The cat sprang toward them but was foiled at the last second—Papa pulled the lid down over them so it lay flat on the ground. The cat batted the edge of the lid, trying to get at them.

"What do we do?" asked Rory. Gran was about to answer, but she didn't have to. The door flung open and the girl's mother came out and scooped up the cat.

"There you are!" she grumbled. "And you're soaking wet!"

As soon as the Human shut the door, Rory and Morgan ran to the lid and lifted it up, whooping and cheering.

"That was close, huh?" said Papa, grinning as his sons jumped up to give Rénaud a paw-slap.

"That cat didn't stand a chance," said Rory.

"Not with us around!" said Morgan.

"I can see life is never boring with you Stowaways," laughed Rénaud. "But where's your grandfather?"

Nobody responded. They didn't have to; Rénaud could see it in their falling faces.

"Let's get home now," said Papa anxiously. "I'm worried about Mama and Bimble. This is no ordinary storm."

A siren grew near, whining like a mosquito through the thundering wind.

"That ambulance is close," said Gran.

"Quick!" said Papa. He led them down the alley to the road along the river. The road was deserted. Only a few parked cars were left to shudder in the wind. Several trees had blown over and were strewn along the bank, their roots heaving up the soil. The ambulance appeared on the Seekum side of the bridge.

"They're heading toward us," said Papa. "When they slow down at the traffic light, we'll jump on. Hurry!"

Everyone ran to the intersection at the foot of the bridge. Rory was getting ready to leap when a deafening crash sounded in his ears, shaking the ground beneath him. He crouched down and covered his head. When he opened his eyes again, everything had changed. An enormous tree had fallen through the telephone wires and blown out the electrical box on its way down to the street, where it landed across the main route out of town.

Every light went out in Eekum, leaving the street in a dark, gray downpour. Whirling red and blue lights flashed as the ambulance crossed the bridge and screeched to a halt in front of them.

Two Humans in uniform jumped out of the cab, wielding an axe and chainsaw.

"Now!" said Papa. They ran under the ambulance and jumped onto the back bumper, where they waited, sheltered from the wind.

When enough of the tree had been cleared, the Humans got back in the cab. The siren wailed once more as the ambulance roared up Main Street and turned right onto the highway out of town.

Rory had never traveled at such a speed. Branches and shingles flew past them, covering the road in a layer of debris. The ambulance clung to the road as it swerved through the wreckage in powerful swells of wind.

His heart pounded as he held tight to the edge of the bumper. But he knew everything was going to be all right now. There were no more secrets and no more lies. He could follow Papa home without having to fight anymore.

His body grew heavy as he closed his eyes and imagined Glasfryn. Mama and Bimble would be at the door, rejoicing as they returned. There'd be a crackling fire in the hearth and a dry bed to fall into. Exhaustion filled his body at the thought. Only one more leg of the journey, and then he could rest.

The ambulance slowed and pulled over.

"Everybody down!" said Papa. They leapt off the bumper and onto the road. "We're lucky they stopped so close to home. I wonder—"

Papa scurried across the shoulder of the road to the ditch they usually crossed into Biggle's farm. Rory followed, trying to keep up. When they reached the gravel shoulder, Papa and Gran shared a look of concern. Water was gushing below them at an alarming rate. Even in a rainstorm, the ditch had never been impassable.

"We'll keep west until we reach the driveway to the petting zoo," said Papa. They followed the road past several ambulances that were parked along the shoulder. As they drew closer to the driveway, they could see the bridge ahead, and the emergency became clear.

The south wall of the bridge, still partially rebuilt, had collapsed. The great mass of rock had fallen into the river and blocked much of the pass underneath. The river was forced sideways and was rising up the banks. A bulldozer had tried to remove the rock, but the machine's mashing crawlers had weakened the bank and now the bulldozer was sinking into the river with the operator trapped inside. Humans in uniform were rushing to the scene.

Just as the Stowaways reached the driveway, another section of the bridge caved in and a wave of water swept over the bank and along the ditch.

"Hurry!" shouted Papa. The wave hit the driveway and washed over it, chasing the Stowaways toward the zoo. Rory took a deep breath as the water circled his feet and rose to his chest. *One more leg of the journey…*, he thought.

Morgan waded past him then looked back in surprise. Rory was usually the faster one. Morgan pulled his brother up to his hind legs. Together they pushed through the wave, which finally petered out at the far side of the parking lot. They stumbled up the grassy bank and under the fence, crossing the muddy pigpen and deserted stalls, under barbed wire and feeding troughs, until they reached the boat pond on the other side of the zoo.

Rory crumbled to the ground. "I need a rest," he said.

"Me too," said Rénaud, rubbing his wounded leg.

Rory let his body sink in the saturated grass. It felt good to lie down out of the wind. If he could just stay here until the storm passed—

"One minute. Then we've got to go," said Papa, looking anxiously at the pond.

Gran and Rénaud sat next to Rory while Morgan moved toward the bank.

"Stay back," Papa warned him. The rain had filled the pond like a bathtub ready to overflow. Water had already risen over the dock; the toy boats had come off their moorings and were swirling around in chaotic loops. Morgan pointed at one boat floating close to the edge.

"It's heading for the old streambed!" he yelled, running around the pond.

"Be careful!" Papa called after him before turning back to Rory. "You ready to go?"

Rory sat up. His head was pounding. *Only one more leg…*

Papa continued slowly so Rory could keep up. He could barely see Morgan through the driving rain that now seemed to splash up from the ground. They had almost caught up to him when they were blocked by a horde of Weedle Mice moving uphill.

"So the townie-lovers return," said a mouse at the front.

"Harry Belter," growled Papa under his breath.

"Where's your wife? Stranded at home?" said Callie, who appeared behind Harry.

"What do you mean, 'stranded'?" said Papa.

"The river is rising, fool," replied Harry.

"But our home is on a hill."

"Take your chances if you want, but we're going to higher ground. Come on, sons." Wally and Dill caught up to their father.

"What's that thing?" said Wally, pointing up at Rénaud.

"It's got a nose like a pig!" said Dill, snorting.

"It's a pig-mouse!" laughed Wally.

Rénaud glared down at them.

"Careful," said Gran, flashing her claws at them. "The monster will chase you if you don't keep your mouth shut!"

"A monster?" squealed another mouse as they hurried away.

"It'll eat us!"

"I knew they'd bring danger back from town!"

"That's the end of it!"

"The Stowaways have finally ruined us!"

Mice trampled around them and scrambled past the "monster."

Rory lost sight of his family in the growing throng of mice. He stayed put until the last mice scuttled off, watching their bodies disappear like bubbles of soap down a drain. He was about to turn, when he saw Tamrin run back a small distance and then stop. She gave him a little wave.

Rory lifted his paw to wave back, but Gran, Rénaud, and Papa moved across his path. "Well, we're on our own, as usual," said Papa, shuffling by. When Rory moved to wave at Tamrin again, she was gone.

Papa looked across to the old streambed, which had begun to flow with runoff from the pond. "Where's Morgan?"

Rory noticed that the boat they'd seen near the edge of the pond was gone, too, but he was too tired to speak.

"He probably just went home," said Gran. "We'll meet him there."

Rory stumbled after Gran, Rénaud, and Papa as they kept to the edge of the stream. It was strange to see their path flowing with water. Something caught his eye over his left shoulder and he turned. Behind them, a yellow-hulled sailboat bobbed up and down as it pushed over the pebbles. A white-hulled boat followed, and then a blue one surged ahead of the others. The stream was steadily turning into rapids. If Morgan had taken the green-hulled sailboat, Rory hoped he knew what he was doing. He was about to yell ahead to tell Papa when his foot landed in water. He stopped and backed up.

"The bog is flooding," called Papa. He was already up to his belly. "We'll have to cross the stream and travel down the other side."

Rory looked anxiously at the rushing water.

"I'll carry you." Rénaud picked Rory up and held him over his head while Gran and Papa waded beside them up to their necks.

They reached the opposite side and climbed the pebbles up the shallow bank. Seconds later, the bog swallowed the stream in a sudden whirlpool, sucking the boats into the reeds. The stream calmed and lowered as the water flowed away. But it wouldn't be long before the water from Biggle's pond flooded the stream again. They ran the rest of the way home.

"Harry was right!" said Papa, stopping at the base of their hill. The natural moat around the bottom was filling with water.

"It's too deep to cross!" said Gran.

"We'll make a path." Papa began to collect pebbles, throwing them into the moat. Everyone followed suit, hurling in stones as big as they could lift until a trail of rock began to surface through the water. Papa hopped over the stones to the other side and ran up the hill toward Glasfryn.

"I'll stay here," said Rénaud, who continued to heave in stone after stone.

Gran followed Papa, leaving Rory behind. He looked anxiously from the bog to the moat. As soon as the bog water crept far enough to join it, their hill would be surrounded. And once Weedle River flooded the bog... His whiskers quivered at the thought.

"Go—get your family out of there," said Rénaud. "There isn't much time!"

Rory splashed across the pebble bridge and up the hill. Papa and Gran were hugging Mama and Bimble at the door.

"Rory!" Mama pulled him to her. "Come inside, all of you."

Bimble threw herself at Rory. "You came back!"

Rory hugged his sister, unable to respond. The happy reunion he had dreamed of was battered by the storm.

"We've got to go," said Papa, who stayed by the door while the others moved inside.

Rory glanced at the kitchen. Their pouches were already stuffed and sitting on the table. He looked longingly at his bed, but he knew it was no use. Though he already knew the heavy feeling of missing home, now that he'd finally made it back, it felt even worse to have to leave again.

"I know," said Mama, squeezing Rory's paw. "We're all packed, aren't we, Bimble?"

"Ready to go," said Bimble, taking his other paw.

"Where's Morgan?" asked Mama.

"We thought he'd be here by now," said Gran.

"He was, but after he said you were all on the way I sent him back outside to double-moor the boat he'd brought down. He told me everything. I'm so sorry about Willis, Gussie."

"There's no boat out there now," said Rory, worried.

Papa clenched his jaw. "Now we have to wait for him."

"Morgan will be fine," said Mama. "He's more than proven himself, don't you think? We'll find him once we're off the hill—he's probably gone to higher ground. We have to leave. Now."

The Stowaways looked around their home one last time. Wind tore at the thatch overhead and rain hissed down the chimney, making the fire smoke and spit. The map began to peel off the wall as water poured down the plaster.

"Goodbye, Glasfryn," said Bimble. Rory squeezed his sister's paw and smiled. She always knew just what to say.

Everyone bustled to put on their pouches and gather outside. Rory hesitated by Grampa's sundial as his family took off down the hill.

"Come on!" Papa yelled back.

Rory took a deep breath and fumbled along, trying to balance his heavy pouch against the wind. When he reached the bottom of the hill, Rénaud was still feverishly throwing stones into the moat. He'd managed to build a wall high enough to form a dam against incoming water, but it was struggling to stay in place. Pebbles fell into the water below, one by one.

"It won't hold for long!" shouted Rénaud. "Hurry!" He crossed the drowning pebbles and held his paw out. Mama took hold of his paw and Bimble took hers and then Gran's, and together they carefully crossed from stone to stone.

A rumbling sound came from Glasfryn. Rory turned to look just as the chimneys crumbled in.

"Go," said Papa, pushing him forward. The flooded bog had reached the moat and the force of the rising water began to push against the stones. Pebbles spun and knocked each other as they moved and settled. Rory put his foot down cautiously on one that looked stable. But as he lifted his other foot to join it, the stone tipped and fell, causing the other stones to loosen. Water surged through the dam, taking Rory with it.

"HELP!" He could barely get the word out before he was dragged underwater. A paw reached in to grab him but slipped off his tail. The sound of the storm grew muffled as his body rolled over and down. The rushing water pulled him around the hill. Rory flailed his arms in an attempt to swim—if he didn't get out soon, he would be taken to the river. But his arms were so heavy and tired....

A stick poked him hard in the belly and soft feathers floated around him. Was that Glee? He quickly grabbed the feathers and let himself be pulled out.

Wind howled in his ears again as he lay face down in the grass, coughing and sputtering until the water escaped his lungs. He turned over and opened his eyes. Papa was leaning over him with Gran's cat-tickler in his paw. Rory smiled faintly. So it was useful, after all.

Papa carried him back over the hill as voices grew louder from across the moat.

"The stones have washed away!"

"Stay there! We'll think of something!"

Papa laid him back on the ground. All Rory wanted to do was sleep. If only he could go back home and crawl into bed....

A loud squawk pierced the wind. Was that a bird of prey? Rory scanned the sky, looking for danger. His mind flashed back to the museum in Seekum—all those wings, spread in flight, wider than their entire hill.

As he struggled to get up, he recognized the white-tipped wings that dropped down beside him. He let himself fall back again.

It was Glee.

When Rory woke, he was lying in a strange bed. Activity shuffled and banged all around him.

"How did you get off the hill?" said a voice.

"A bird carried us away."

"A bird carried us away."

"A *bird*?"

"The one Rory made friends with a while ago."

"So it was true!"

"Thankfully."

That was Papa's voice. Rory opened his eyes, relieved. He was talking to Miss Bucket. But her home wasn't the place of solitude he remembered. It was chaos. Miss Bucket was ransacking her cupboards for food while Aunty Hazel followed her around, talking incessantly about bicycles. It looked as if she'd lost her mind again. Miss Creemore was trying to get Aunty Hazel to sit long enough to strap a pouch around her. Papa and Mama were arguing over how best to re-pack the pouches, while Bimble drew a picture on the table, as calm as could be.

Rory sat up. On the table beside him a candle had melted down and dripped all over the floor, but no one had bothered to clean it up. Something bad was happening. And where was Morgan?

"What's going on?" he said.

"Good," said Papa. "You're up. We've got to get moving."

"Again?"

"The river's still rising. It won't be long before it floods the tunnel. Rénaud and Gran are keeping watch on the plateau outside."

Rory couldn't believe it—how could the river have risen so high? "But...but what about Morgan?"

"Glee went back to look for him."

Rory slipped out of bed and moved to the door, looking anxiously up the dark tunnel. He didn't want to lose his brother now; they'd only just been reunited. He couldn't wait to tell Morgan about all his adventures with Gran. And this time, he knew his twin would listen. It was like the minutes between their ages didn't matter anymore—they had somehow become closer, and yet more different...

When he turned back to the room, everyone was staring at his feet. A pool of water had collected around him and was now spreading over the floor.

Gran blew past him through the door. "Everybody out!" she shouted before running back up the tunnel.

Mama ran out after her, her shoulders hung with the rest of the pouches. Miss Bucket and Miss Creemore grabbed Aunty Hazel's elbows, helping her up.

"Careful, puppets—that's two of four limbs I have to carry me out of here!"

"Can you run by yourself?"

"*Can* I!" Aunty Hazel raced out the door in front of them, her stubbed tail wagging behind her. Papa picked Bimble up and ran on his hind feet with her in his arms. Rory went out last, wading through the water as it poured down the tunnel, the force nearly sweeping him off his feet.

The plateau outside was already under water. Papa splashed

onto the stairs, climbing after the others up the cliff. Bimble held tight around his neck.

Rory dug his claws into what was left of the staircase; the rain had pounded it into a lumpy trail of mud. He looked to the sky, hoping for a change, but the day had only grown darker. Would the storm ever end?

"AHOY!"

Rory stopped and searched for the voice in the wind.

"Down here!"

He looked below and there was Morgan, poised at the bow of the green pond boat, its white sail glowing against the steel gray water. Mack was at the wheel.

"Help!" Mama's voice squealed from above. "The stairs are washed out—there's no way up!"

"Get everyone down here," said Morgan, tying the boat to a root jutting out of the cliff.

"We can't all fit on board—," began Rory.

Papa turned back and grabbed his arm. "What are you doing? Move higher!"

"It's okay, Papa. Look!" Rory pointed below.

There wouldn't be enough room for everyone in the boat, but that didn't matter—Morgan had rounded up the rest of the boats and tied them, stern to bow, behind him.

Glee squawked overhead and flew away.

·୧ EIGHTEEN ୨·

DESTINATION UNKNOWN

Dawn was surprisingly calm. The chain of boats drifted downriver, heading east through the forest, their colored hulls growing brighter as the sky lightened. It was a welcome change from the blindness of the night before.

After they had boarded the boats, they'd untied from the drowned cliff and lassoed the rope to a fallen tree that drifted past, hoping it would jam between the bridge posts downriver, where they could climb along the trunk and onto shore. But when they reached the road bridge, it was only a pile of rubble, abandoned by the Humans. A sudden whirlpool caught the tree, forcing them to untie and let it go before it smashed into the rocks. The string of boats was carried over narrow rapids, pulling them helplessly down into the river beyond. Everyone was drenched but alive, their tails coiled tightly around the masts as the boats struggled to stay upright. Too far from shore and too tired to think, they had huddled in groups, trying to sleep as the wind howled on through the night and the boats were swept downriver.

The storm had finally blown itself out and the sun was rising for a new day, but Rory still couldn't relax. He leaned over the stern of the last boat in the chain, watching the water churn in its wake. They had lost so much in so little time. What would they do now?

The boat moved through a giant patch of red cranberries floating on the surface like a slick of bubbly, red oil. Rory reached in to pull one out, but his paw caught on something bobbing underneath. It was Mama's thimble pot. He plucked it out quickly, using it to scoop out a cranberry. Taking a bite, he chewed the sour flesh as he put the thimble down on the deck beside him. There would be no turning back now. Glasfryn was gone.

Gran moved to sit beside him, leaving Rénaud to sleep near the mast. Rory handed her the cranberry to share. She bit off a piece and munched it hungrily.

"Mother Nature is wild and woolly, huh?" she said with her mouth full. "She cradles us to sleep and then *kicks* us out!" She was trying to be funny, but Rory didn't feel like laughing.

"Mmm," he replied, distantly.

"Your grandfather and I lived through several hurricanes before you were born, you know. Even before Papa was born."

"Yeah?"

"When we lived farther west."

Rory looked up, disbelieving. "Glasfryn wasn't always our home?"

Gran smiled. "Of course not! Life is always changing. We had to move downriver as towns grew up around us. The whole lot of us Weedle Mice used to travel together, but I guess those days are gone. I don't suppose they'll miss us, do you?" She laughed.

Rory smiled. They were leaving so much behind, good *and* bad. He wished they could have taken Grampa's sundial, though.

"So I guess we'll find a new place to live, huh?" he said, feeling a bit better.

"Without a doubt," said Gran.

"And we'll go on adventures, like always. Right?"

"Would we have it any other way?"

"Papa might."

"I dare any one of us to defy the Stowaway spirit again!" She put the thimble on her head, making a grumpy face like Papa might have made when it fell on his head at the farm.

Rory laughed. That day seemed like so long ago. He already missed the farm, the school, the bog, their home....

Gran saw him sadden again and she put the pot down, rustling around in her pouch.

"I did manage to bring one thing," she said, and placed something in his lap.

"The book of fables!"

"I found it at Miss Bucket's."

Rory flipped through the pages. Some were stuck together with water, and he closed it quickly before he ruined it. He was excited to read the rest when it dried. It was clear he belonged to a lively breed of mice, who might merit a fable or two—he had a feeling there might be more tales within that had been inspired by his ancestors. He put the book inside his pouch.

"I brought something, too," said Rory, suddenly remembering. He pulled out the gnomon claw he'd snapped off the sundial. "To remind us of Grampa."

Gran took the falcon's claw, looking at it proudly. The tip was broken but the talon was strong.

"We'll make a new sundial when we get to wherever it is that we're going," she said. "But whether or not we have things to remember Grampa by, he'll be with us, always." She covered her heart with her paw and gave the claw back to Rory.

Rory smiled, putting the talon inside his book as a marker. He began to think fondly of all that had happened in the past few months. There had sure been lots of scares and doubts about his family, but he *did* feel a little wiser. He picked up his tail. The last ring was fully darkened now. He was about to show Gran when her head slumped down on his shoulder.

Rory helped her move next to Rénaud, where she wrapped her tail back securely around the mast and settled down to nap. Rénaud jerked awake.

"W-where are we?" he stuttered, looking in alarm at the churning water.

"Don't you remember what happened?" said Rory.

"Ah…yes," said Rénaud. "Well, things could be worse—at least we're not in a cage!"

"Not that you'd be any help if we were," murmured Gran, with one eye open and a smile creeping over her face. Rénaud laughed.

Rory moved to the bow and pulled on the painter until the stern of the next boat came close enough to climb on. It was Mack and Jack's red boat he'd watched from a distance all that time ago. He hopped over and let the rope go, and the last boat fell behind again. He crawled across the deck toward the bow.

Jack was snoring loudly over the wheel. Aunty Hazel was sprawled out with Miss Creemore and Miss Bucket's tails wrapped around her ankles, holding her on the teetering deck as they all slept.

"A thousand boats for a bicycle," mumbled Aunty Hazel, rolling over. She was either seasick or had definitely lost her mind again. Rory bet on the latter.

The next boat was empty. The mast was cracked and half of the rail was ripped off; it wasn't safe for passengers. Rory inched carefully across to the next boat in the chain, where Mama and Papa were huddled together with Bimble asleep in Papa's lap.

"Come sit," said Mama, waving Rory over. He sat down beside her and she pulled him close. "I would have waited forever for you to come home, hurricane or not. I missed you so much."

Papa ruffled the fur on Rory's head. "He's a brave one. We'll have to keep our eye on him now."

Rory tried to smile but a yawn overcame him, causing Papa to yawn, and then Mama. They all laughed.

"Where do you think we'll end up?" said Papa.

"Doesn't matter. As long as we're together," said Mama.

Rory agreed. Wherever they built a new home together, a garden would grow up around them.

The boat jerked to the portside and Rory looked forward. Morgan was on the next boat, testing a new painter he'd braided out of reeds, pulling on it hard. Rory left his parents and Bimble to sleep and jumped over the bow to join him on the leading boat.

Mack was half awake at the wheel and nodded to Rory as he went by. Morgan climbed up the mast to clean the shredded leaves off the sail, peeling them off and pitching them overboard. Unlike everyone else, he didn't look tired at all—he was enjoying his role as captain.

Rory moved to the bow and stood on his hind legs, holding onto the rail. The air breezed through his fur. The river was wide and they were well away from shore, moving at a swift pace. It would be impossible to tack against the current. They would have to wait, maybe for days, before they could land.

Devastated banks passed by in the distance. Wharves were thrown up over the land among dozens of boats, their deep hulls exposed like beached whales. Rory wondered how far past the drawbridge they had gone. He must have been sleeping when they passed it—the last place at the edge of his parents' map. Maybe they were well into the World Beyond now. But he didn't think it was a place where Terrible Things happened—maybe it was a place where Terrible Things *could* happen, but didn't always. After all, they had met a great friend in Rénaud, and that was a wonderful thing.

Bright sun warmed the roofs of the tattered houses. The air was calm and light. Their boats were sailing easily and would be for a while. It was a good time for a nap. Rory was turning around to go back when Bimble pushed her nose under his arm.

"Oh, hello, where'd you come from?" Rory smiled.

Morgan came down from the mast and lifted Bimble onto the rail, holding her tight. Her ears blew back in the breeze.

"I drew a picture for you," said Bimble, pulling a piece of paper out of her pouch. She passed the drawing to Rory, who shared it with Morgan.

"That's where we're going," said Bimble.

"Oh, really?" said Rory, laughing.

He'd never seen anything like it. She'd drawn hills towering in the sky and covered in snow, and birds as big as goats soaring over deep gorges and waterfalls.

"Wow—how did you imagine all that?" said Rory in disbelief.

Bimble hesitated before answering. "I dreamed it."

Rory stared at his sister. She still didn't say much, but she definitely wasn't a baby anymore—she'd grown to twice the size she used to be. Though funnily enough, her ears didn't seem any smaller.

"You're an original, Bimble," said Morgan, giving her back the drawing. "I've never seen a mouse so focused."

"Like you and your bike?" said Bimble.

"You had a bicycle?" said Rory, astonished.

"Well, I made one, but it fell apart."

"I missed a lot this summer!" said Rory.

"Where'd you go?" said Bimble.

Rory wasn't sure where to begin. "It's a long story," he said finally.

A gust of wind blew Bimble's ear across her face. "I'm all ears!" she giggled.

Rory laughed. "Well, it looks like there'll be lots of time for telling stories." Up ahead, the river widened into a clear blue sea.

Morgan took a deep breath. "We're going on a *big* adventure!"

ACKNOWLEDGMENTS

Most of all, I thank Mum and Dad for building me shelves and filling them with books when I was young, for taking me on adventures in the World Beyond, and for giving me space and time to write.

I thank my lucky stars for: Jill MacLean, whose generous advice led to the publication of this book; Ann Featherstone, for telling me what my story was about and for her kindness and joy throughout the editing process; Gail Winskill, for believing in a first-time novelist like me and giving *The Stowaways* an especially beautiful chance; Dean Griffiths, for drawing mice that make my heart smile; and Rebecca Buchanan, for the sweetest design.

Heartfelt thanks to: Jed MacKay, for understanding my vision, however foggily it began; Jodi Reid, fellow explorer, for comic relief and leadership; my writing group—Judith, Val, Brett, Susan D. and Sheila—for sincere encouragement; my costumer friends and book club, for cheers and support; Kymn Keating, Trevor Murphy, and Faythe Buchanan, for infectious enthusiasm! Margot Aldrich, for delight in the good things; Sam Fisher and Ben Zelkowicz for inspiration, near and far; Gail Swingler, for the worlds we created as children; and Brian Lindgreen, for a constant shoulder, level head, and warm heart.